Match, Cinder & Spark
Volume 6

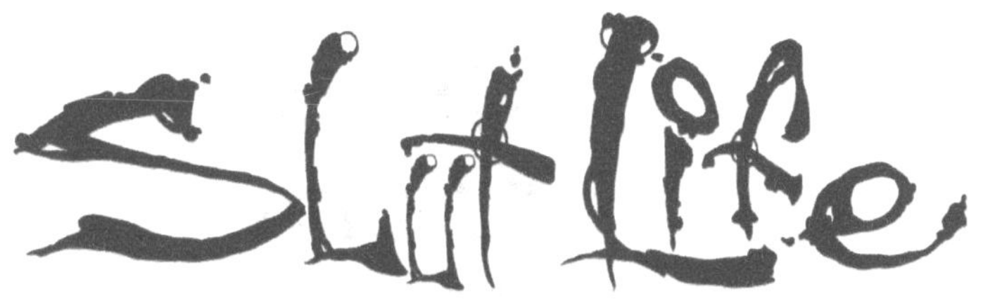

A Literotica Roman à Clef
By H.H.

An imprint of Erosetti Press
ErosettiPress.com

ErosettiPress.com

Follow Us & Subscribe

ErosettiPress.com

Podcasting on
all platforms!

Contemporary &
Classic Literature

Dedication

For Lola, who has ever reminded me of Aphrodite, born of the sea

"I don't want the only conversation about female sexual desire to be about consent. Consent is incredibly important, but it's not the only word. There is also such a thing as female desire that has its own impetus that's not just about a woman waiting for a man to come to her and ask for something, and the woman decides whether she will give it or not. Female sexual desire is a muscular, dangerous, dark – and I don't mean sinful, I mean primal – urge that is just as difficult to grapple with as male sexuality. And it exists. And efforts to sanitize that are going to be futile."

Elizabeth Gilbert
Interview with N.P.R.
"Weekend Edition"
June 8, 2019

Table of Contents

Preface: A Report on the Nymphomaniac Condition

It was said by the renowned sex researcher, Alfred Kinsey, that "A nymphomaniac is someone who has more sex than you do." It would seem that modern psychology has caught up with Kinsey's insight. The dictionary of psychological disorders, the American Psychiatric Association's Diagnostic and Statistical Manual (DSM), removed nymphomania from its list in 1980. But does that mean Nymphomania no longer exists?

In popular culture "sex addiction" has been used as a catch-all for a number of "disorders" that have been named and described: hypersexuality, compulsive sexual behavior, erotomania, hyperfilia, etc. But the DSM puts almost all of these under one listing: Sexual Disorder Not Otherwise Specified. This heading is as ambiguous, amorphous, and as slippery as the subject itself.

However, let's keep in in mind that no matter how something is categorized or listed, it's not a "disorder" unless it is distressing to the person exhibiting it or has detrimental effects in one's life. If the result of the behavior is a net negative, then it could be labeled a disorder. That net negative could be manifested psychologically, as in feelings of guilt and remorse, or could result in actual physical harm to oneself. Other net negatives could include weakening of relationships, loss of a job, or other harms external to oneself.

In modern European and American culture, nymphomania has as checkered a past as the women diagnosed with it. Even though there is a male correlate to it – satyriasis – the two labels have been employed in radically different ways. Historically, the ascription of "nymphomaniac" has been applied to women who, had their gender been ascribed to men and the behaviors described as those of men, rarely would they be described as afflicted with satyriasis. In other words, historically, women exhibiting the same healthy and robust sexuality of men would be diagnosed with a disorder while their male counterparts gained the praise and admiration of others as Don Juans.

But, in the last decade or so, with the rise of internet porn, the term "sex addict" has been increasingly utilized in less stereotypical and gender specific, patriarchal ways. Famous actors such as Rob Lowe, David Duchovny, and Charlie Sheen all have come out as being sex addicts, making it easier for others to do so.

Despite the DSM debunking the myth of nymphomania and our modern society's willingness to embrace a more gender-neutral term applicable to men and women, the term "nymphomania" and its connotations continues to live on in the culture's consciousness and the collective unconscious.

Nymphomania is a concept that has a history to it almost as old as civilization itself. In Jewish lore there was Lilith, the contemporary or predecessor of Eve, who refused to be subservient to Adam and, supposedly, insisted on taking the "top" position during sex. Her name is derived from the Hebrew for "night" and she is associated with other female night demons who seduce men. As such, she is a succubus. This tale probably has its origin in explaining men's nocturnal emissions.

Throughout history, assertive women and sexually promiscuous women have been associated with the demonic. Accusing a woman of being a witch was one way of marginalizing or eradicating powerful and lustful women. In more recent times, diagnosing them as hysterical was another. Perhaps if we rewrote history as "hystery" (from the Greek, hyster, meaning "womb"), we would have different stories to tell. But, from the ancient

Mesopotamian Epic of Gilgamesh, in which the goddess of love, Ishtar, unsuccessfully tries to seduce the hero, and the temple prostitute, Shamhat, successfully seduces and thereby defiles the natural man of the wild, Enkidu, to Helen of Troy, whose face and unfaithful figure launched a thousand ships, to the Sirens and Calypso, all the way through to Gatsby's fair Daisy Fay Buchanan, wanton women have been revered and rebuked by the West's confused attitude toward female sexuality.

In the West, only Virgins, like Mary, and doting, devoted wives, like Penelope and Henry James' Isabel Archer, get univocal approval.

(The East, by contrast, is not as uncomfortable with strong, sexual, and wise women. From Kali to Guan Yin, not only are they revered and worshiped, but even the gender ambiguity of Vishnu is given prominence.)

Even in the contemporary medium of myth-telling – movies – the nymphomaniac is never depicted as anything but pathological and her fate is always a morality tale told from the point of view of the negative exemplar. Lolita, the touchstone of our modern-day horny heroine, has been made into a movie twice: once in 1962 by Kubrick and once in 1997 by Adrian Lyne. Based upon the classic book by Nabokov, the films and the book stand in a league of their own. The ultimate fate of Nabokov's Lolita (spoiler alert) is morally ambiguous. Clearly a letdown to the pedophile protagonist, Humbert Humbert, when he finds his life-long love at the end of the book, we are never given any insight into mature Lolita's feelings of fulfillment in family or lack thereof. However, it is, perhaps, too hasty to say that there have only been two Lolita films made. One of the most popular tropes in porn is Lolita. In this way the myth of the nymph lives on and on.

Other films, such as Lars von Trier's Nymphomaniac and Craig Brewer's Black Snake Moan, put nymphomania front and center. However, in both, the female protagonist is depicted as pitifully damaged and pathologically in need of redemption. In the latter film, that redemption takes the form of Christina Ricci, dressed only in her panties and a cutoff t-shirt, being chained to a cast iron heating radiator by a strong black man (Samuel L. Jackson). As psychologically dubious as this "treatment" might be, it could be said that the film gets to some deep, underlying archetypical images and fantasies buried in the American collective unconscious by playing on race, gender, and slave tropes.

The former film, Nymphomania, as drab and sexually non-stimulating as it is, does get to some diagnostic characteristics. As Robert Weiss, founder of the Sexual Recovery Institute, has discussed in his "Thoughts on Nymphomaniac: Volume I," in the Huffington Post, March 20, 2014:

Nymphomaniac: Volume I is "sex addiction accurate."

• Joe's sexual exploits start out (rather early in life) as innocent and fun-seeking, but before long she's using them less for enjoyment and more for escape. This is typical. Simply put, addicts of all types engage in their addictions not to feel better, but to feel less.

• Joe views men as objects -- a means to sexual gratification -- rather than seeing them as equals and potential partners in emotional intimacy. When her lies actually ruin one man's life, she feels nothing for either him or his wife and kids. Nor does she change her behavior.

• Joe spends nearly all of her free time pursuing sex. She has no other interests or hobbies.

• Joe's sexual activity escalates in both amount and intensity. She has more and more partners as her addiction progresses, and she engages in ever-more risky behaviors.

• Joe's response to any sort of emotional crisis is sex. When her father is terminally ill in the hospital, she has sex with an attendant. Later, she experiences sexual arousal at his deathbed.

• Joe seeks a sense of control and power through sex. For instance, she 'allows' or 'forbids' certain activities. At one point she speaks to Seligman about 'privileges' granted to one of her regular sex partners. Using sex to feel 'in control' is common with sex addicts, especially with female sex addicts.

• Joe appears to have not bonded appropriately with her 'cold hearted bitch' of a mother, relying on her father for kindness and nurture. Her childhood flashbacks show that she learned ways to 'please' her father, and that doing so was incredibly important. Even though their relationship does not appear to have been sexual or otherwise abusive, it is clear that she learned early on that the way to get love from men is to please them. This type of dysfunctional childhood bonding is common in sex addicts of both genders.

• By the end of the film, Joe's entire life (not just her sex life) has become 'monotonous and pointless.' She compares her daily movements to those of a caged animal. Everything she does is rote and repetitious, and nothing has any meaning – especially not the sex. At one point she says to a partner, during sex, 'I can't feel anything,' and it is clear that she is talking about both physical numbness and emotional numbness.

Though Weiss points out in the article that female sex addicts are often ascribed "highly shaming labels" such as nympho, slut, tramp, and whore, "that society routinely attaches to women who have a lot of sex, regardless of whether they do so because they enjoy it" or not, he does not in any way discuss the possibility of a positive nymphomaniacal experience in which those labels are coopted into accolades.

The linguist Geoff Nunberg has pointed out that many one-time derogatory and profane words have been coopted and reappropriated by the subjugated, marginalized, and oppressed populations against whom the slurs were originally leveled. As he says about the term "slut," "after a Toronto police constable told a crime prevention meeting that women should avoid dressing like sluts if they don't want to be victimized," "slut walks" served as a way "to protest the whole culture of slut-shaming." He points out that, "it is hard to imagine 'slut' being reclaimed the way 'queer' was, as a respectable label for academic programs and cultural centers" ("Slut: The Other Four-Letter S-Word," on Fresh Air, WHYY, NPR, March 13, 2012).

This sort of reevaluation of values is exactly what Lo is literally embodying, pushing psychology today to free itself from the prejudices of patriarchy. She wears the labels "slut," "tramp," "whore," and yes, "nymphomaniac", proudly (and she often wears little else). Between us, we use the words "nymphomania" and "slut" as honorifics rather than stigmatizing terms. Every slur can be reclaimed and used subversively by the oppressed.

There is some evidence that lustful, liberated women are making inroads into the tyranny of normativity. Thinkers such as Rollo May have proposed a theory of the daimonic, hearkening back to the origin of "demonic", as coming from the Greek "daimon." For the Greeks, daimon meant something more akin to a personal deity; a guiding angel, you might say, rather than a guardian angel.

May uses the term "daimonic" to denote a drive that is not univocal in nature and, in one word, is akin to Freud's dual Eros/Thanatos drives. As May says of the daimonic, it "has the power to take over the whole person. Sex and eros, anger and rage, and the craving for power are examples. The daimonic can be either creative or destructive and is normally both." (May, Rollo, Love and the Daimonic, p. 123)

It is worth mentioning here that, before May and Freud, there was a theory of human psychology in Judaism that posited two chambers in the heart: the yetzer tov and the yetzer ra. The former, "the impulse for good," and the latter, "the impulse for evil," worked in tandem and the rabbis believed that neither was "evil" (unlike the proverbial Christian good angel and devil on one's shoulders), but that the yetzer ra was a force that propelled humans to creativity and sexual union, but it needed to be bent toward the yetzer tov in order to avoid its destructive tendency and be sublimated into socially acceptable expressions and activities that benefited society. One can easily see the parallels between that and Freud's Eros/Thanatos theory. Perhaps "parallel" is too benign. Maybe Freud was more plagiarizing from his own tradition. In line with this theory of complementarity, May has said, "The daimonic (unlike the demonic, which is merely destructive), is as much concerned with creativity as with negative reactions." (Diamond, Stephen A., Anger, Madness, and the Daimonic: The Psychological Genesis of Anger, Madness, and the Daimonic, from the Forward by Rollo May, p. xxi)

In the nymphomaniac, the daimonic drive has been described as a propensity toward indiscriminate, compulsive, and often risky sexual behavior. To the extent that this is dangerous, harmful, and results in negative net results, it is "pathological."

But that's not the whole story.

As was mentioned above, the daimonic is also the engine driving creativity and the nymphomaniac can use her prurient powers for good, positive, "healthy" outcomes. As Mihaly Csikszentmihalyi, the pioneer psychologist in the study of "flow" or "optimal experience," has said, "One manifestation of energy is sexuality. Creative people are paradoxical in this respect also. They seem to have quite a strong dose of eros, or generalized libidinal energy, which some express directly into sexuality." (Csikszentmihalyi, Mihaly, "The Creative Personality," Psychology Today, 1996, p. 38) I believe that the reverse of this is true as well: One manifestation of sexuality is creative energy. Perhaps that is because, as Csikszentmihalyi also says, "a certain spartan celibacy is also a part of [the creative person's] makeup; continence tends to accompany superior achievement. Without eros, it would be difficult to take life on with vigor; without restraint, the energy could easily dissipate." (Ibid.) Of course, the nymphomaniac is characterized by her lack of "continence," but that does not mean that her prodigal participation in pleasure isn't also a creative, artistic, and perhaps even a performative act. Seeing sex and art as two separate realms is the fundamental error in this analysis. Sex can be every bit a creative endeavor, full of "flow" and genius as a Picasso or Pollock painting. The only difference being that the "results" are fleeting, ephemeral, perhaps even "dissipated."

In my case, I would say that writing about Lola Down, my own personal high priestess of porn and beloved nymphomaniac, is also a result of the daimonic and the writing often flows of its own accord in peak moments, like autographia. According to Csikszentmihalyi, flow is the experience of intense concentration during creative endeavors. For me, that describes the act of writing. For Lo, that describes the act of fucking. For me, the restraint and "continence" is crucial to produce just the right amount of effulgent energy. But for Lo, her creative power may be more akin to "the woman who identifies with the archetypal role of Muse or femme inspiratrice, providing sexual love to artists" (Diamond, Stephen A., "What Motivates Sexual Promiscuity?" Psychology Today, 2011).

This is not to say that Lo doesn't have her own creative endeavors, her own talents, interests, and areas of outstanding achievement. Far from it! But she does love being celebrated as muse, not only by me, but by all the artists who have been inspired to draw or paint her, as well as those who have written lovely verse and prose to her and about her. In addition, she frequently hears from women and men and couples who credit her as an inspiration in the bedroom. Frequently these accolades are accompanied by "tribute" photos of the men, women, and couples cumming to her inspiring images.

As much as all this worship is proudly welcomed by Lo, it is also of concern how many people – mostly men, but some women – write in to lament that, for them, the nymphomaniac is akin to some sort of mythical figure, a unicorn, a phoenix, or the Holy Grail. These awestruck admirers cannot believe that one exists, in the flesh, as it were. They had heard rumor of such creatures, but had never met one or received confirmation of their reality. Lo, like the Holy Grail, is for them a receptacle into which they can pour forth all of their hopes and dreams (and bodily exuberances) and also a cup that runneth over, spilling forth for all who thirst for her baptismal water.

Is this perceived paucity of nymphos due to the stigma attached to the term, repression of sexuality, or a failure to recognize and reclaim the term in a positive light? I don't have the answer to these questions, but one thing was clear early on in my relationship with Lo – I was unable to find authors writing about their nymphomaniacal girlfriends and the great challenges such relationships entail. So, I began writing about our relationship in a public forum in order to inform others and also to find out if others could inform me. It's been a fun and enlightening journey and I thank all of you for your words of wisdom, encouragement, and envy. But most of all, I thank Lo for opening me up to all new vistas of life's possibilities.

Summer Lovin'

It was the last week of summer camp and after a long hot August of teasing the other counselors, Lo was eagerly looking forward to the final day and night of "Counselor Camp Cleanup." Lo had been going to this camp, tucked away in the remote mountains, since she was in pigtails and denim shorts. She loved it. It was her only respite from the teasing of school and the oppressive torment that was home. It's where she developed from an awkward adolescent into an off-limits tantalizing temptress. It's where she learned first-hand to French kiss, where she discovered the power of a sheer white bikini, and where she fell in and out of "love" on a weekly basis.

It's where she and her like-minded girlfriends stole a ladder from the supply closet and scaled the wall of the boys' changing room to spy from the gaps in the rafters on those mysterious hard-body wonders as they showered after the morning athletics hour and before swim time. It's where she gossiped at night with her girlfriends in the bunk about what base she had been to with which boys and what it was like. It's where she kept hidden her secret attraction to the girls and desperately sought private time to satisfy the constant gnawing and craving between her legs. It's where she admitted in confidence to her best friend that she liked to touch herself and where that best friend outed her to chants of "slut" and "queer" from her peers. It's where, out of pure self-preservation, she learned to live out the cruel labels of the girls and, through that, discover the complex psychology of the female mind.

Each year she rose up through the ranks: from camper to CIT (counselor in training) to head CIT and now, too old to be a camper, she had gotten her first summer job at her favorite refuge from "real life." She knew from previous years' chats with the counselors she flirted with that once the campers returned to their hamlets after their tearful good-byes and the camp was populated only by the counselors who worked there in order to tidy it up and tuck it away for the winter, that that was when all the weeks of flirtatious eyes, silly and childish pranks, and salacious innuendo culminated in a naughty, naughty night of skinny dipping, naked relay races, strip poker, fondling by the camp fire and fucking in the woods. Lola couldn't wait! Neither could the guys who had had their sights set on her all summer long.

You see, Lola and her friend, whose name was, quite appropriately, Summer, had dedicated themselves to taunting the guys with their flirtatious antics. They had solemnly sworn to each other an oath of "No Boys!" before camp even began. This was prudent as well as playful, for any counselors caught "fraternizing" with the opposite sex were swiftly and immediately shipped home without pay. Curiously, there were no rules about "fraternizing" with the same sex and so Lola and Summer kept each other in line by exploiting this loophole in the rules to the greatest extent possible – frequently in eyesight or earshot of the guys they wished to torture exquisitely for sport.

But now, on this Bacchanalia night, the impossible would be possible. The girls had worked themselves up into a frenzy just whispering about it to each other under the sheets after lights-out all summer long. Having built up the momentousness of the occasion in their minds since first hearing rumors of it years ago, they could hardly contain themselves as first one and then the other traded fantasies of what would come.

When the last day of counselor camp was upon them, the first eight or so hours fell far below Lo and Summer's expectations. It was filled with orders barked at them from the headmaster to clean the latrines, scrub the mess hall, sterilize the kitchen, and do strenuous lifting and pulling of heavy equipment from the grounds to the shed. Lo and Summer kept up each other's spirits until finally the last dish, last bunk, and last hammock was stacked, stored, and folded for the winter.

It was 6:00 and there was still about an hour of good daylight left. Now that the campers were all gone, the counselors, for the first time that summer, could crack open cold bottles and cans of beer as they sat around the campfire and barbecued their dinner together. But during that odd hour with the sun descending and casting magical light across the valley where the camp was nestled, the counselors didn't feel so much frisky as literally "fraternal." The camaraderie among them never felt so strong as it did then, reminiscing about the past summer with its mishaps and highlights. All the counselors felt a pang of love and nostalgia for the campers about whom they complained all summer long, but whose absence they now keenly felt with bittersweet sentiments. It was a quiet and reflective time watching the fire burn brighter as the sky grew darker.

But then, as they laughed and delighted in making their S'mores, a feeling of sexual energy filled them as if Aphrodite herself had cast a spell upon the shadowy circle. Lo and Summer weren't the only female counselors among them, of course, and slowly, one-by-one, different guys and gals paired up and drifted off into the night. However, the women were outnumbered by the men and before too long the circle had reduced itself down to just Lo and Summer and six guys, all of whom had designs on one or both of the ladies.

The eight of them talked and eventually someone brought up the often-observed hole in the wall of one of the boys' cottages. "The Glory Hole" was the joke that circulated since time immemorial. Banter went around the campfire that that was just a legend. Others fervently disputed that claim. Finally, Lo said, "Let's check it out." Everyone got up and went to cabin #3 of the boys' side of the camp and, at first one of the guys stuck his fingers through the wall on one side saying, "See, it could be big enough!" as Lo and Summer grabbed the fingers on the other side as if they were giving a hand job.

Then Lo got on her knees and put the boy's fingers in her mouth – deep into the back of her throat. "Wow!" came the call from the boy's side.

"It's just the right height!" Lo called back.

And then, as you might expect, one of the daring boys – encouraged no doubt by a summer of celibacy – put his long, thick cock through the half-dollar sized hole.

"Who is that?" called Summer.

"Guess!" was the response.

Lo took the delicious looking cock in her mouth and out rang the question, "Who is that?" from the guy on the other side.

Both Lo and Summer replied in unison, "Guess!"

The game went on for a while with the guys and gals taking turns until first one and then another exploded, and then each in turn, like popcorn, went off. Eventually they all had their chance.

When they emerged out of the cabins, the women were more eager than ever to be satisfied.

"Rope!" said Lo as she looked at the neatly coiled cords they had put in the corner after untying the volleyball net. Summer and Lo looked at each other and knew instantly what the other was thinking.

Lo slipped out of her shorts and her shirt, and, with a bit of encouragement, she and Summer convinced one of the guys, who was supremely able with his knotting abilities, to tie Lo down to one of the cots. Summer slowly removed her own clothing, and she tested the waters for the guys.

This little performance was enough to revive their spent energies and when Summer saw this she said, "Who's first?" They all clamored to be first, but Summer picked one and, with ease of hand and nimbleness of fingers, she slid a condom on his cock. "Have her," she said as she guided his cock between Lo's spread legs. Summer, for her part, straddled Lo's face and held the young man's cock as he went in and out of Lo.

Lo screamed with delight and when the first participant was done, all she said was, "More!"

One-by-one the guys took turns with Lo until each had her ... twice.

"What about you?" said Lo to Summer when she realized that they had nothing left to give her.

"Lo," said Summer, whispering in her ear, "I never wanted them. I just liked hearing you talk about it. It's you I've wanted since tenth grade."

Summer untied her beloved and the two of them went back to their cabin where some of the other counselors were in bed with their various lovers. They got naked in the moonlight and slipped into bed together and Lo never slept as soundly as she did that night, held tightly in the arms of Summer.

Jealousy

It was Lo's graduation from her master's program and festivities were in order. Most of Lo's grad-school friends were, like Lo, only a couple years out of their undergrad and all her grad-girlfriends were, unlike Lo, planning on celebrating this momentous event with their parents. Of her many friends, Lo has four with whom she's really bonded during the brief couple of years she's been doing her coursework. These four – also quite interested in sex, sexual health, and women's issues – formed, with Lo, something of a *Sex in the City* quintet. They frequently met for coffee and talked about sex, dating, relationships. They went out to clubs together. All of them are attractive, but for one reason or another, only Lo is in a long-term relationship – albeit an open relationship. Other than the fact I am almost twice Lo's age and Lo participated in some rather kinky experiments – all in the name of good scientific research! – at the behest of her friend Valery, Lo's coffee clutch grad cohort is ignorant of her nymphomaniacal tendencies. That is, other than what they may suspect or infer, they do not have first-hand knowledge of Lo's insatiable needs, her frequent "deviant" indulgences, or her exhibitionist qualities. I don't doubt that these young and lusty ladies haven't suspected Lo of unabated lustfulness, but to be fair, each of them most certainly carries a hidden (or not-so-hidden) freak-flag themselves.

I mention all of this by way of introduction to the events of last weekend – graduation weekend. The ladies – Valery, Stephanie, Linda, and Camille – made plans for a swanky lunch at an exquisite French restaurant where the parents would join (and pay). Lo has been estranged from her parents since her freshman year in college. She has avoided any and all contact with them and, at this point doesn't even know if they still live in her childhood home and she sure as hell hopes they don't know where she lives.

Earlier that day Lo and I had had a little lovers' quarrel. The details of the spat are unimportant, but the upshot of it was that Lo apologized to me profusely and she wanted to show her penance in a tangible way. I told her that there was one way for her to redeem herself. "Anything, Daddy, anything," she said, with a knowing look in her eye.

I lived up to her expectation when I said, "Tonight we're supposed to have dinner with your friends and their parents."

She nodded her head in anticipation.

"First, you must wear something *scandalous.*"

"Like what, Daddy?"

"I'll leave that up to you, but there must be no doubt that it is scandalous."

She nodded in obedience.

"Second, you must not wear panties."

Her lips were now licking the front of her teeth in that excited, hungry sort of way she has.

"Third, you must wear your Ben Wa balls."

"Lovely, lovey!" she squealed.

"And lastly, you absolutely must, must call me 'Daddy,' at least once in front of your friends. I don't care how you manage to do it, but you must say it audibly."

She then pouted. "No spanking, Daddy?"

She turned her little bum 'round for me and showed me where to spank. I gave her a good whack that must have stung more than she expected, for she showed me a real pout after that as she rubbed her sore bum.

I went out to do some errands (including buying a graduation card and chocolates) while my little vixen got herself all dolled up for the evening. When I returned to pick her up in front of the apartment, I swear people must have thought I was a John picking up a trick. Lo was dressed in a very high hemmed black little number and a partially see-through white top made of tattered yarn. Yes, she wore a black bra under it, but that didn't prevent her from looking perfectly scandalous in her black pumps.

She hopped in the car and I said, "Hey sexy."

"You like, Daddy?"

"MMMM, hmmmm," I hummed.

We drove to the brasserie and our table was reserved on the second floor. It was a steep walk up and Lo, knowing that her little skirt couldn't conceal her exposed puss, waited till everyone else had gone up before ascending the stairs with me right behind her sweet behind. I watched as her seductive snatch squirmed its way up each stair with a little twist between her luscious legs. Barely visible at certain moments was the string of her Ben Wa balls peeking out every now and then. Just as I was thinking that it was good that no one was behind me, a waiter started going up the stairs. No doubt he had as good a view of Lo's sweet spot as I, if not better!

So, there we were, sitting around a long table set for twelve. You see, Valery's mom is divorced and neither she nor her mother speak to her father. Only Stephanie's mom flew in for the celebration – too expensive for both parents to make the cross-country flight. Both of Linda's folks were there, as were both of Camille's parents.

After some introductions, we sat at the candle-lit table and made small-talk as we enjoyed the delicious baguettes. Wine was eventually served, followed by appetizers, dinner, and much more wine. After everyone had had about three or four glasses, including a glass of champagne for a toast to the graduates, what started as a stiff and uncomfortable assortment of people grew into a warm and genial group whose barriers of difference melted away under the influence of alcohol like ice walls under a warm rain.

Between courses, my right hand slid its way down under the table to Lo's knee and slowly worked its way up her leg to her warm inner thigh, where I discretely fondled her clit and found my way to her Ben Wa string. I tugged on it gently, just to get the balls bouncing against each other inside her. She squirmed in her chair and looked at me. One time she almost made a little jump. I continued to touch and tease her every chance I got. Every once in a while, I noticed Stephanie's mother – a tall woman with long auburn hair – smiling at me behind Lo's back. She sat to the right of Lo and it made me just a little self-conscious. Could she see my right hand fondling Lo's lap? Was she flirting with me? I put these thoughts aside and forgot about the curious smile as I imbibed the wine and allowed the delicate flavors of the French cuisine to excite my pallet.

The meal was delicious, and the conversation was enjoyable; however, since for every dance the piper must be paid, eventually the steep bill came and each of the young ladies – eager to get out into the working world, but, as of yet poor as church mice – turned to their mother or father and looked pleadingly or appreciatively for one last show of support. One of the fathers scrutinized the bill carefully before begrudgingly paying his share, another put in what was asked of him, the two mothers gladly contributed to the kitty, and Lo, well Lo looked to me.

It was at that moment that it struck me – I'm not a boyfriend out with his girlfriend! I'm closer in age (and status, responsibility, and looks) to the generation of parents than to the generation of graduates. For the most part, Lo makes me feel twenty years younger. But every once in a while, there is that ah-ha moment when I realize how grossly mismatched we must seem to outsiders.

I gladly collected all the cash in the overstuffed leather-bound check-holder and replaced it with my Gold Card – the symbol of bourgeois respectability and financial security. (Little did anyone suspect the real situation of my finances at the time!) Lo looked to me with gleaming admiration and I must admit that her love and esteem make any price to pay worth it a million times over.

After the waiter took the check, Lo leaned over in her chair and gave me a sweet peck on the cheek and whispered in my ear, "Thank you, Daddy." I gave Lo a knowing look that said, "Audible."

She turned to everyone at the table and said, "I know a great Italian pastry shop just down the street from here where we could get some sweets." She then turned to me and said, just as loudly "Do you want some, Daddy? I mean, 'sugar daddy.'" Everyone laughed and all said that Italian confections would be the perfect way to complete the evening.

We got up and made our way down the narrow streets. We started in pairs, with Lo on my arm, but then different people wanted to talk with different combinations and Lo moved ahead of me to talk with Valery and Linda. I ended up walking and talking with Stephanie's mom, named Debbie. I could tell that she was slightly inebriated and that the wine had loosened up her lips. She was telling me all about how proud she is of her daughter and how everything is so wonderful, except that she would love for her daughter to find "some good man, someone she could really love." She went on to say how wonderful it is that Lo and I are together and how it would be great if Stephanie could find "someone like you – older, more mature, good looking." She flattered me. I flattered her right back with compliments and praises – for her and her daughter. She asked how Lo and I had met and that led to a discussion of how I was Lo's professor once upon a time. She delighted in the scandal of it and began saying how she would totally fall for a professor like me, "I mean, back when I was a young college student."

Before she could say any more, we were at the patisserie, and I was tempting Lo with all sorts of delicious delights – cannoli, cake, Italian cookies. She settled on the cannoli and, as we all ate our treats in a large circle on the street corner, Debbie and two of the other three moms were fawning upon me as Lo stood next to me. I could tell Lo was growing jealous of these ladies who were clearly vying for my attention. But, at the same time, perhaps even imperceptibly to Lo due to her own jealousy, I was aware that these ladies were jealous of all that Lo had going for her – a new graduate, young, beautiful, care-free, and with an older gentleman whisking her away to different destinations in and out of the city each weekend. Oh, how they wished to trade places with Lo, even for a day!

After everyone had finished dessert, Lo and I sauntered back to our car. My hand around her back slowly slid down, inch-by-inch, till it was resting on her bum. It didn't stop there, but continued till it was slightly pulling up the bottom of her skirt, revealing a crescent of the moon.

She smacked my hand down, and, as I helped her into the car, I smacked her bum hard. I walked around the car and got in the driver's side, and before I was even fully behind the wheel, she lunged at me, kissing me open-mouthed, her skirt riding up to her hips as she clumsily straddled the stick shift. I struggled to pull her off and said, "WHOOOA!"

"Daddy, I wanted you all night," she said as she made another foray to get on top of me. Again, I pushed her back and said, "You just get in your seat, little girl, and let us get out of here."

She pouted but sat.

"Let's go dancing!" she said, squirming in her seat.

She recommended that we go to a place on the outskirts of town, and I began driving us there. Before we had hardly gone down two corners, she was frantically fingering herself in her bucket seat. She moved her left leg up and over the stick shift and had her legs spread wide as she grabbed my right hand and placed it between her legs. "Finger me, Daddy. I'm *so* horny!" I followed her instruction. She was wet and her pussy lips were spread wide, and I could feel one of the Ben Wa balls right on the edge. I pushed it back in and did my best to curl two fingers up inside her. She moaned and moved her torso to fuck my fingers, rather than my finger fucking her. She maneuvered her right leg to put it up on the dashboard and used both her hands to push and pull my right hand in and out of her pussy. She came a couple of times like that.

She then reconfigured her position and leaned over, undid my belt and pants, pulled out my cock and started blowing me as I drove. Her head bobbed up and down in my lap as I tried to keep my eyes on the road.

As we pulled into the parking lot of the dance club, rather than get out of the car, she practically jumped into my lap and lowered herself on my hard cock as her skirt slid up like a belt around her waist. She bounced hard, up and down, between me and the steering wheel.

She came again. Then she turned around and faced out the front window as she bounced in a reverse-cowboy position on my lap. She watched as people walked by in the parking lot and she moved her hands up to her breasts to pull and pinch her nipples. She came a couple of more times that way.

Finally, after drenching my pants in her wetness, she said, "OK, Daddy-O, let's go in."

"Lo, I can't go in like this! Look at me. It looks like I spilled a bottle of wine on my lap!"

"Never mind that," she said, "It's dark in there. No one will ever know. Button up and let's go dancing."

I did as she wished and before long, we were in the dance club.

The music was blasting that horrid THUMP-THUMP-THUMP-THUMP, like the regularly recurring pounding of a pile driver. No matter, Lo went and did her little dance. It was so loud in there that she had to scream to tell me, "I love dancing with my balls in!" She kept dancing as I went to the bar to get us drinks. When I came back to the dance floor, what did I see but Lo grinding (or rather, being ground) between two men. I just took in the view and drank my drink. Slowly, I noticed, her little skirt was being lifted by the close friction of the guy behind her. He held her by her hips and skillfully shimmied the skirt up inch-by-inch. Before long, he was cognizant of Lo's lack of undergarments, and he turned her around so his friend could see as well.

Lo just played along. When the unbearable thumping of the bass and drums came to an end, only to be replaced by more thumping and pounding, Lo came up to me and took her drink. The guys followed. I was not going to scream introductions, nor did I care to hear their names. So, I just smiled politely and suggested we leave after our drinks. Lo pouted again and mouthed "Daddy," amid the noise. I saw her talk to one of the guys – "whispering" (that is, screaming) something in his ear. He, in turn, said something to his friend and, after a moment, they both nodded "Yes."

Lo finished up her drink and we started to go to the door. To my surprise, when we got to the door, both guys were behind us. When we stepped outside into the relative quiet, Lo said to me, "I told them we would give them a ride back."

"Where's back?" I asked.

"Wherever you're going," said the taller of the two guys.

They got in the back seat, Lo sitting between them, and I started driving us home.

Lo lost no time in making out with one and then the other of the boys. I couldn't see in my rearview mirror, but I'm sure each of them had his hands on her legs and elsewhere. Before too long I saw Lo's head going down first this way and then that. Then I could see Lo sitting straight up. I turned my head and glanced in the back seat when I was at a red light. She was giving each of the guys a hand job – stroking up and down with both hands like a skier using her poles – as they fondled her pussy. She came a couple of times and then the guy on her right came all over his lap. This allowed Lo to focus on the guy on her left and she leaned over, wrapped her mouth around his cock, and went to town. Eventually he blew his wad in her mouth and on her face. When she was done, she said, "Right here, Daddy. This should be fine."

Both guys got out of the car and Lo rejoined me in the front seat.

"Lo," I said.

"Yes, Daddy?"

"You were a *bad* girl."

"I know, Daddy."

When we got home, I told her to take a long, hot shower. I heard her cumming in the shower and I thought, "How much can this girl cum in one day?!" When she came out, I asked her, "Do you still have your balls in?"

She nodded, "Yes."

I told her to get on all fours. When she did, I told her her punishment is to give me her ass. As I began pounding her, she stuck her hand in and fondled her balls, bringing herself to her final orgasm of the night before begging me to make her my little cream pie. Try as I may to punish her by withholding the object of her desire, I couldn't help but to give her what she wanted.

The House-Call

Morning. Silence. The sun has not yet risen. A bird chirps alone outside my window. Probably a baby bird waking its mother, no doubt. Hungry. In the dim stillness the sound of my fingers on the keyboard pecking away as I compose yet another ode to Lo. My e-mail is open, hidden behind my Word screen. I hear my computer chirp its own hungry sound as something arrives in my in-box. Who could be writing to me now at this ungodly hour? I check it out. There's a missive from Lo, short enough to have been straight out of the period of Morse Code. "I require laying." Stop. That's all it says. I now know she's awake in the bedroom. Horny. Wet. And wanting. I ponder the possibilities a moment. Do Lo and abandon my story of/for her, or ignore her and ... Wait. There's another chirping from my computer. Another telegram from Lo. "And/or a set of Double A batteries." I search. There's a pair of Double A's in the remote. I take them out and go to Lo.

Cracking the door, I see her naked body silhouetted against the pale window of the bedroom that faces east and the sunrise. She smiles, mischievously. But it's not such a mystery what she wants and what makes her smile. Her hands are at work under her hips, manipulating her clit. "Here are your batteries. I'm writing," I say with a faux dismissiveness.

"Oh Daddy," she begins in her pleading whisper, "But I'd so much rather have you."

"Nothing doing. I haven't had my coffee yet."

She rolls over with a sigh and a pout.

I return to the quiet of the living room, but I'm distracted by the silence. I listen intently. A minute. Two. Three. Yes, there it is – the sound of Lo's orgasm. Didn't take long. I know she's being loud purposefully. It's her mating call. It's her Siren song.

I play with the thought. Yes. Yes, that's good. I like that. The thought, that is. I'm imagining what devilish fun it would be to deny Lo my manhood for a week and only indulge in interludes with her in my imagination. Deny her all physical pleasure. Deny myself as well. Mainly it's the self-denial that allures me since I am intrigued by the thought of restricting my indulgences to only my words. But the thought of Lo going out of her mind with distraction delights me. Spare the rod, spoil the child. Is that how it goes? But with Lo it should be: Spare the rod, cajole the child right into temptation. Yes. What *would* she do? Jill it? But of course. Would she be reduced to taking ads out on Craigslist again? Calling strangers? Going down on men at clubs? Oh, to what depths will she plunge?

I decide this *is* a good week to deny her.

After her orgasmic groans fade away, I walk down the hallway to my little insatiable nymph and crack the door. "Lo, I'm telling you right now; I'm on the wagon."

Swooooosh! She throws a pillow at me! I duck out of the way just in time. She pouts again and says, "Fine! I don't need you." She pulls out her little silver bullet battery operated vibrator and her ginormous red dildo and begins going to work on her puss a second time. All before sunrise, mind you.

When I get undressed to take my shower, she sits on the edge of the bed and fondles herself as her tongue glides over her sparkling teeth, her lips parted. I deny her.

When I get out of the shower, wet and dripping, she is on all fours on the bed, first facing me and then turning around wagging what would be her tail at me, naked, fingering her pussy and ass, enticing me to come to her with my glimmering cock. I deny her.

When I get dressed, she thrusts her hand down my pants. She grabs and says, "Oooh, Daddy." I deny her.

During the day I get texts and pictures from her, showing and telling the nasty things she's doing alone at home on the bed. I ignore her.

When I get home and pull the belt out from around my waist, she says, "Spank me Daddy, I've been bad." I refuse her.

When she makes my dinner, she does so naked, taking every opportunity to bend over. I admire her.

When she sits down to eat, she pulls my foot up between her crotch to feel her wet pussy. I admonish her.

When we sit down on the couch and watch TV, she spreads her legs before the bay windows. I can't help but look at her.

When she pulls and tugs at her pussy lips and asks me nicely to pet her, I can't help but to give in to her.

When she fingers her pussy and asks me to lick her fingers clean, I acquiesce to her.

And then, then, just when I'm on the brink, her phone rings. Who is it, but Sylvia. Lo says, "Oh, hi." Pause as Sylvia says something. "Oh no, we were just on the couch watching TV. Don't worry. No you're not interrupting anything." Lo talks as her fingers fidget up and down the length of her pussy. I get on my knees on the floor and push her fingers out of the way and take her luscious, large pussy lips in my mouth and I lick them up and down, just as she was just doing for herself with her fingers. Lo's head drops back. She continues talking. Nothing arouses me as much as Lo's voice. I hear her sighing but trying to keep the conversation going. Sylvia is going on and on about Clyde. I don't know what she's saying, but Lo, instead of ushering the conversation to a close, encourages the girl to go on ... and on. I lick, I suck, I nibble, and Lo is squirming on the couch, a small puddle accumulating on the leather. She turns to the side to sigh and let out a small scream. She whispers to me, "I'm cumming. Yes, Daddy, I'm cumming. Stop. No, I need you to stop." Stop is supposed to be our safe word, but there are strong stops and soft stops. This is a soft stop. I continue. She cums – all over my face.

When she is done, she gets off the phone and says, "Have me, Daddy!" I deny her.

After a lot of back-and-forth of the same, she finally stomps off to the bedroom, grabs her 16-inch dildo, and hops in the shower. After a few minutes, she screams in such a way as to make up for the swallowed orgasm she had on the phone. When she gets out of the shower, she exclaims to me, "I think I just fisted myself for the first time!" When I ask her to show me, she shakes her head and says, "Oh no, Daddy, you have to fuck me first." I deny her.

Day two and day three continued in much the same vein. But on the fourth day, she said to me, "Daddy, remember how you promised to get me that massage last Christmas?"

"Yeah, Lo, I remember," I said. "Well, I want it now."

"Lo, that offer was only good till the end of January."

"NOW, Daddy!" she demanded.

"OK, ok," I said.

"But I want it to be a man and I want him to make house-calls."

I got on the internet and did an extensive search of Lo's strict criteria. (Oh, yes, there were more exactitudes about what was acceptable to her.) Finally, I found one: a certain Mateo. He came highly recommended. I made the arrangements, but he couldn't book Lo till the next afternoon.

That night I fell asleep – or was well on my way to falling asleep – when I was startled by the weight of Lo's naked body on mine as she whispered in my ear, "Do me, Daddy. Do me."

When I realized I was no longer dreaming, I said, "No, Lo. Go to sleep. Now!"

Two or three more times that night I felt her naked body gyrating to the rhythmic pulsing of her large purple dildo pounding her pink pussy repeatedly in the darkness as she watched a video on her phone and called out, seemingly to no one. But I heard her and, much as I resented being woken from my slumbers, my member sprung to action with delight at the sights and sounds.

"Do me, Daddy. Do me!" Her mantra.

"No, Lo. Go to sleep!" My mantra.

The next day, Saturday, Lo didn't get out of bed. She lay in bed laying herself all morning. Only around 11:00 – an hour before her appointment with Mateo – did she finally emerge from the sheets and blankets to walk five feet to the shower where she cleansed the cum from her thighs, fingers, and every place else she happened to hit while squirting in the bed. Of course, she took full advantage of the double-showerhead to bring herself to a window rattling orgasm.

Ding-dong. Yes, just as she was cumming in the shower, the doorbell rang and there was Mateo – all six-feet-one of him in his finely pressed white knit shirt and black jeans revealing just large enough of a bulge to drive Lo mad with manlust. I let him in, shaking his hefty, meaty hand as he grinned a pearly-toothed "howdyado" at me that brought out his dark Mediterranean complexion. "Lo will be a minute. She's just ... er, finishing up in the shower."

As I made clumsy excuses for my little vixen, she called out from the bathroom down the hall, "Holy fucking shit that was AMAZING!"

"Lo," I called back, as I walked briskly to the bathroom door, she had left ajar, "Your masseur is here."

"Oh, well, send him right in," she said as she stood naked, dripping on the bathmat, only a towel loosely draped over her hip.

"Lo, you have to put on clothes."

"Fiddle-dee-dee," she said, in a conscious and silly imitation of Scarlet.

"Madame will see you now," I said to Mateo, in a conscious and less amusing, rather creepy imitation of Max Von Mayerling from *Sunset Boulevard*.

In went Mateo with his box of tricks and his folding massage board to the bedroom (that still reeked of Lo's late night, early morning masturbatory exercises).

I sat in the living room impatiently trying to keep myself occupied. I picked up a book and then tossed it on the chair. I picked up another book and immediately shut it. I listened intently. No sounds, and then her flirtatious chuckling.

I turned on the radio, but was instantly annoyed by the fact that it made it impossible to eavesdrop on the bedroom. I paced. That didn't help. Who knows how much time went by? No, that's a ridiculous rhetorical question. I know *exactly* how much time went by. Twenty-five minutes. Then I heard Lo moaning. It could have been that Mateo – *MATEO* (stupid name) – had just magically unlocked Lo's trapezius and the relief was overwhelming. But let's be honest here, shall we? The reality probably was that he unlocked Lo's trap alright and she was moaning in delight.

At forty-five minutes, she was indubitably screaming with orgasmic pleasure. And at fifty minutes, all was silent. By this point, I realized I was a precious few feet away from the bedroom door. I heard a thunk of the box and I made long, ballerina like, tip-toe strides away from the bedroom and back to the living room.

Soon Mateo emerged from the bedroom and Lo followed, holding her white towel up over her bare breasts and revealing ever so slightly the tip of her triangular temptation. Mateo walked right up to me, and, for a moment, I thought to myself that he was expecting me to slap him on the back and congratulate him for a job well done, but then I came to my senses and realized that this was a business transaction and he was waiting, grinning of course, to be paid for his services. I dug into my pocket and fumbled out my fat wallet and counted out the twenties to pay him, adding an extra one on top for tip.

Off went my good boy to the next house-call on his list and my little Lo stood in the hall grinning for a moment before turning tail like a little bunny and scurrying off to the bedroom where she waited for me with open legs. I gave her what she wanted – a good lay – and she gave me what I wanted – the blow-by-blow.

I was lying on top of her as she was in the missionary position, and she whispered into my ear as I gently plunged my throbbing knob deep inside her. She said:

He started by massaging my feet. He began with my toes – each one individually with his special lubricating oils. He had the firmest, yet delicate fingers and he knew just where to place them on my toes. He then circled round-and-round my heel and worked his way into my sore ankles. Slowly he worked his way up my calf (each leg individually, of course) and to my thighs. He took his time with my thighs, rubbing them with both hands, kneading them like dough. More than once I could feel the tips of his fingers treading dangerously close to my ass and just grazing the glistening lips of my pussy. I had the towel draped over my back as I lay on my tum, but I'm sure it was high enough that he could see *exactly* where he was going to go next. Even though I had jilled it all morning, I was aching for more. I wanted those strong, tender hands to fondle me, finger me, fist me ... if I could stand it.

But he was *very* professional. He continued massaging my thighs for a long time, teasing me as he made a bit of small-talk. Asking me if I jog, telling me that my legs are beautiful but tense. Oh, I was tense alright. I was aching for him. But he then moved to my back, abruptly skipping the part of my body that most needed a massage. He stood in front of my head and leaned over deeply to get the small of my back. As he did so, I could see the bulge in his jeans and, not wanting to embarrass him, I put my head down into the towel. He leaned so far over that the bulge gently bumped my head and I could feel how strong and solid he was. His hands went way down into the small of my back and under my towel to the top of my ass. Back and forth he went with long, deep strokes gliding over the warm massage oils. Back and forth and, as I felt his cock pressing on the top of my head, I almost came right there. But he slowly began working his way up my back to my shoulders and neck. He went to the side of the table and his pulsating hands cascaded their relaxing movements from my neck all the way down, first one arm and then the other. I felt as if I was turning to jelly, but all the while I was dripping on my towel thinking about the package he had in his jeans.

He then asked if I wanted to roll over. I complied immediately, allowing the towel only to cover my hips. This time he began with my shoulders and worked his way down my arms again. But soon he asked if I would like to have my entire torso rubbed down. I nodded in agreement with this suggestion. He put a puddle of oil in the palm of his hand and slowly worked his way down my shoulders to my breasts and ever so gently caressed them and squeezed them. When he heard me moan and saw my response, he gently tugged at my nipples and pulled at my breasts, asking, 'Does that feel good?'

I could hardly speak. He knew it felt good and he continued down my tum. When his hands got to the towel, he politely asked if he could remove it. I nodded, 'Yes.' He took it off and saw my cleanly, sweetly shaved pussy. My pussy lips must have been pink and glistening from the shower and all the self-manipulation I had done that morning. He was so professional! He didn't say a word. He was again standing by my head – this time I was facing up, right at his crotch – and he leaned forward and gave me a good deep rubdown from my tits to my pussy, and as he did so his package went right into my face.

'You can do that again,' I said, and he leaned over again.

'Again,' I said.

He repeated the gesture.

'Do you want to get out of those jeans?' I asked.

Without a word, he unbuttoned his jeans and let them down. I reached up above my head and pulled down his tight undershorts and out sprang his giant cock into my face.

'Try it one more time,' I asked.

This time when he leaned over me, I took his cock in my mouth, and he continued leaning as his big fingers found their way to my wet and waiting cunt. He fingered me as I sucked him off for a good long time. But then I pulled at his rod, and I said, 'You know, I have some talents of my own.' I flipped over and my face was exactly the height of his amazing member. I took it, deep into the back of my throat. It was a good nine inches, I'd say. I just opened up and let him stick the entire thing as deep as he could go.

He pulled out and said, 'I'm supposed to be giving you the massage.'

He moved to the middle of the bed, used a lot of oil all over my clit, pussy lips and ass and began massaging everything all at once. I came and came hard within seconds. I squirted, Daddy, I squirted all over that poor young man's hand. He didn't seem to mind. I asked him if I could return the favor by sucking on his cock and he ever so politely told me that unfortunately our hour is over and he must be on his way to his next appointment. 'Perhaps next time,' he said.

After all those days of denying my little trollop pleasure, I was excited and tense and hard beyond belief. As I listened to her story, I had to keep backing away from the edge and slow things down to get through the entire account. But when she was done, I told her to put on her glasses.

"Why Daddy?"

"Just do it, damn it!" There was no time for explanations.

She did as she was told as I continued doing her and then, once she had them on, I pulled out of her and moved in one jerky motion to her face and ejaculated all over her glasses, face, and hair. She was a happy whore – my little Lo.

TCB on Vacation

Each year in the fall, after the prime season is over, but while the air of summer still lingers, Lo and her best girlfriends from college rent a house on the beach. The vacationers – mostly those families with kids who are pegged to the school calendar and so can't stay past Labor Day – are gone, but the water is still warm and the days still long enough to enjoy the sandy beach in the morning and afternoon and the clubs at night. Plus, the peak prices of summer have been cut in half, so the ladies get the hot spots all to themselves on the cheap.

Well, this year was no different than those in the past, with a few exceptions. The ladies, five in all, are now in long-term relationships, of various degrees of seriousness. One is married. Three of them are engaged. That leaves just Lo and me as the outliers – still dating, no ring. Because of these commitments, the ladies, for the first time ever, agreed to bring spouses/significant others along. Unfortunately, due to my work and parenting schedule, I couldn't accompany my Lo on her post-summer vacation for the Wednesday, Thursday, and Friday leg of the trip, but I did arrange so I could at least be out on the sandbar for Friday night into Saturday. To keep expenses even lower, they rented the house for only one peak weekend night (Friday) and with only four bedrooms.

Because of Lo's temporary single status, she drew the short end of the stick and was relegated to the pullout couch in the living room. Even before they all embarked on their adventure, I could tell that this was destined for dissonance, if not disaster. Lo's not accustomed to having people walk through her sleeping space at all hours of the night to get to the kitchen or the bathroom and she certainly is not a morning person. So, with eight other adults and one dog (Ruggles) sharing a one-story house with four bedrooms off of one central living room (Lo's quarters), through which one must pass to get to the bathroom and kitchen, etc., I predicted that I would be rendezvousing with one very grouchy Lo on Friday night.

I'll skip through many of the details, mostly because I was not there for the swimming, the walks on the beach, the catching up with each other, the getting to know the spouses better, the silliness, the nights out, etc. Basically, each night at around one or two in the morning (depending how late everyone stayed up drinking and talking, playing cards, or going for midnight swims), I would get a phone call from Lo reporting to me in muffled tones the day's activities.

She told me of the various gossip being shared by the girls with each other about the other girls. We could just imagine what they had to say of us! She told me about how lovely the weather was, where they went for dinner or what they made for lunch. She told me about various hot men and women she saw on the beach that day and how much she missed me. And then she would tell me how wet she was for me, for my cock – for any cock really. There she was, lying naked in her pullout couch, the central room of a quasi-hexagon, spreading her legs, touching herself, begging me for a story. I would slowly unravel a lurid tale as I listened to her moans on the other end of the line. Of course, the sound of her sexy voice brought me to attention, and I would be indulging myself on my end of the line. And then the line would sound as if it went dead. I would sit in the darkness wondering until, after a few moments, Lo would return and say, "Oh, Daddy. I'm sorry. I had to put a pillow over my head. I hope I wasn't too loud. I hope no one heard me. I *so* needed that."

Later, in the dark of the night, I was woken by the vibration of my phone. Groggy, because still half asleep, I heard Lo say, "Daddy, can you tell me another story?"

"Another?"

"Please."

"What have you been up to ..." looking at the clock and trying to calculate how much time elapsed since we last said goodnight "for a half hour?"

"I've been a bad girl," Lo said.

"What have you done?"

"Oh, Daddy, I was masturbating again, trying to cum a second time, but someone walked in on me. It's so frustrating here! Please, just tell me another story. It doesn't have to be long."

And so I began telling her something but, in the middle I heard her say, "Just telling H.H. about our day."

And then she said to me, "Sorry, Daddy, again, someone was walking through. Can you tell me the story via a chat?"

So, I hung up with her and pulled out my computer and we began chatting. I was typing in a fabulous little fantasy (Lo particularly likes fantasies that are about her and involve her being fucked by many men, sucking them off, and generally being the giver and receiver of all their sexual energy) about Lo and the college football team. Something about her going into the lockers with them as they showered and stripping down naked to shower with them as they stood around her and took turns using her mouth before taking her into the gymnasium, laying her down on one of the thick gymnastics mats and taking turns double-teaming her. Occasionally Lo would type, "Yes," or "Oh yes," or "More," or "I like that." But then there were no responses for a while. I knew, or thought I knew, what was happening. Either she was interrupted by another somnambulist, or she was cumming.

Turns out, my guess was correct; it was the latter.

"Thank you, thank you!" she wrote, before writing, "Love you, Daddy. Goodnite."

The next morning, around nine, I got a text from her saying, "Grrrrrrrrrrrrrrrr. I just want to sleep!"

I wrote back, "Morning sunshine!"

She texted, "People have been up and about since seven! WTF?!"

I was at work when she was texting this to me. A few minutes later I got a text that read, "Everyone is up now, except me. I just want to sleep."

And then about 30 minutes later, so almost ten o'clock, she wrote simply, "TCB'd." This is our code acronym for either "Taking Care of Business" or "Took Care of Business." Viz., masturbated.

I immediately texted back, "What?! How? Where?"

She texted to me, "Right in bed with everyone around. They're so busy making breakfast and preparing lunches for the beach that no one was watching me. They thought I was asleep. At least I hope so!"

Such an insatiable little nymphet! But I should have known she'd be up to something like that since this is pretty much the only way she can wake up in the morning.

The next night it was much the same as the first, but this time she included a new detail from her day. She said that the house they were renting has an outdoor shower for people to use when they return from the beach, before going inside. She told me that the house is set on a hill and that the shower is connected to a little deck on the side of the house, but because of the hill, the deck is above the shower. She said that when she went into the shower, she saw that Dan, the husband of her girlfriend Val, was on the deck and was able to observe her in the outdoor shower. She went on to say, again in very hushed tones since she was at the vortex of all the bedrooms, that she could have showered in her bikini, but knowing that Dan was there, she chose to take it off. When she reached up to hang it on the hook, she could see out of the corner of her eye that he was watching her. She lathered up, rinsed off, and then sat on the small, built-in wooden ledge of the shower, put her legs up on the other side of the wooden stall, allowed the hot water to pulse down on her pussy, and began masturbating. It only took a few minutes before she came but, not satisfied with such a quick one, she did it again. From behind the spray of the shower she could look up at Dan, whose eyes were transfixed upon her, without his seeing that she was aware of her audience. After about fifteen minutes of intense rubbing and fingering, she finally came again.

You can imagine how fervently I wanted my Lo as I heard this story. And, to make my position even more difficult, she brought herself to another orgasm by recalling the event for me.

Friday morning, I received another text from Lo. This time it said, "TCB," meaning, she is, as she texts, engaged in the act.

A few moments later I received the message, "Finished."

That was followed by, "Hurry up and get here. I need a layin'!"

Within minutes I was in the car and on my way out of the city. I still had a pile of work to do, but I declared it a half-day Friday. I drove like mad through the burbs and countryside, over the bridge and to the resort town where Lo and friends were staying. I had one hand on the wheel and the other on my hard cock, just imagining all the things Lo had told me over the past two days and thinking about how much I miss the warm, soft, inviting, welcoming, yearning touch of her flesh, her smooth skin, her pearly white teeth, her curly, soft hair.

Topless-Beach Reading

When I got to the sunny beachfront house, four of the ladies were out on the beach, each a cocktail in hand, as the fellas were drinking beers by the grill along with Sally. A small pup tent was set up in the sand for Ruggles the dog and he was quietly enjoying the gentle breeze as the girls talked in quiet voices, punctuated by frequent laughs and giggles. Lo was reclining in her beach chair wearing a cute white bikini, her eyes hidden behind her big, Jackie-O style dark sunglasses and shaded by her large pink beach hat. (A side note here: The wonderful thing about her white bikini is that both the top and bottom become slightly transparent when wet, such that her cute little butt-line, the slit of her pussy, and her nipples are all visible to the discerning observer.)

I bent down to kiss her hello and she responded, "Hello, darling," with a British affectation in her pronunciation. She peeked her eyes over the brim of her glasses and said, "Get out of those clothes."

I looked back at her and said, "You want me naked, right here and now?"

Her tongue grazed the front of her pearly whites, over her lips, and with her eyes she said

"Yes," but her words were, "No, silly! Get inside and change into your bathing suit."

I turned to follow her command and she shouted at me, "Oh, and fix yourself a drink. And one more for me!!!"

When I returned, drinks in hand, suited for the ocean, I pulled up a beach chair next to my Lo. The ladies were involved in a discussion about their summer beach reading. They mentioned this novel and that, but, as with every conversation in the summer of 2012, invariably the topic became the ubiquitous *50 Shades of Grey*. Lo and I have discussed this phenomenon quite a bit. When it comes to literature, Lo can be quite the snob. Not anywhere as snobbish as I, but don't ever dare to say that you think Dan Brown is a great writer or, God forefend, Stephanie Meyers! You will incur the loathing of Lo. Not all modern popular novels are panned by Lo, but the poorly written ones are scathingly critiqued. As far as *Shades* is concerned, Lo is disgusted by the enormous popularity of this – let's face it folks – mediocre, mild-mannered erotica.

I, on the other hand, am perplexed by its popularity, but I do not begrudge it the success it has received since it has been, or may be, the gateway fiction that does for literotica what *1984* or *Fahrenheit 451* did for science fiction. Not that *Shades* will become standard high school reading, but it may just legitimatize the genre, or at least open the publishing house gate keepers to better authors of erotica. It also may serve another important role: opening otherwise inhibited women/couples to explore possibilities they may not have ever even imagined on their own. However, I must admit, I have not read the book. When I want erotica, I turn to the classics: Lucius Apulius, Li Yu's *The Carnal Prayer Mat*, Sappho, The Song of Songs, among others.

Lo's friend Kaylee said she had not read the book, but to her surprise her mother *had* and – she giggled as she said this – recommended it to her. She couldn't get over this and, for that very reason (the source of the recommendation) she felt that she couldn't read it.

Lo's other friend Val, a heavy-set blond woman who is married to the voyeur, Dan, rebuked Kaylee and said with enthusiasm, "Oh, you must read it! You'll love it! I've read the whole series," and then she blushed (perhaps as she recollected in her mind the specifics of reading it). Now, though Val is a bit heavy, she carries her weight in an impressive manner – proudly wearing a bikini and walking with the confidence of a Gaston Lachaise statue created in the image of his muse, Isabel Nagle. Her ample, powerful flesh commands attention and respect, yet her cute, almost cherub like face and blond curls suggests a sweetness and femininity befitting her friendly and happy personality. She projects an innocence and purity that is in contrast with an almost imperceptible deviant strain that most people would overlook, but keen observers with similar freak flags, people like Lo and me, pick up on. So, it was with a bit of embarrassment that the words escaped her mouth about the dark and salacious *Shades*.

Not to worry, Val, because your friend Erin eagerly agreed with you and immediately sat up from her reclining, sun-tanning position, and said, as her eyes lit up, "I did too! I *never* thought I'd be into *that* sort of thing – you know – but it was *so* good." She was practically touching her pussy over her bikini bottoms as she said this; she was so carried away with her excitement. And, from what she said, it was difficult to tell whether the read was so good or trying it out at home was so good. Maybe both.

Lo cast a knowing look at me that said, "Amateurs." I responded with a reserved, hidden, knowing smile. We just listened, curious as to how these newbies to erotica understood it and we weren't disappointed because as soon as Erin said it, she asked, "But do you think that so many women have a desire for *all* of that?" Erin had a way of emphasizing many of her words accompanied by exaggerated facial movements.

"What do you mean?" asked Kaylee.

"The spanking, the rider's crop, the ..." she paused and looked up at me. My privileged position as a fly-on-the-wall for this "gal-chat" suddenly became conspicuous, but the cat was out of the bag now and she had to finish her sentence. "The Ben Wa balls?"

The girls all giggled, that is, except for Lo who just smiled and squirmed a little in her chair. "Lo," said Kaylee, "this is your field. What do you think?"

Lo looked around and then back at me and said, "There are statistics out there on this stuff. The numbers showing women experimenting with S&M, anal sex, and other types of kinks are, in my opinion, incredibly low. I mean, anecdotally speaking, my experience has been that far more than 11 % of women engage in S&M, or 40 % of women in anal sex, or 60 % of women masturbate; at least among women in their 20's and 30's."

The girls laughed and poked fun at Lo's use of statistics and then they joked about "her experience," since, in her coy, scientific way, she totally avoided saying what *her* experience was. Someone repeated, "But what do *you* think. Do women really like all that?"

Confronted with the teasing, Lo simply said, "I know I do" and she looked lovingly at me. Now it was my turn to blush.

This gave the girls pause and then Kaylee, looking back over her shoulder, said in a hushed tone, "I wish Cory would be a little more adventurous in the bedroom with me."

Cory, Kaylee's boyfriend, who was over by the grill talking with Sally, Jeff (Sally's boyfriend), Dan and Steve (Erin's boyfriend), is a twenty-something black man with a great build (he was a running back on his college football team) and a friendly smile. The ladies all leaned in closely to hear what Kaylee had to say. She continued in almost a whisper. "It's always missionary position with him. Occasionally he might take me from behind. But I'd like him to do something more ..." she was struggling to find the right word, "crazy," was all she could find.

"But he's *so hot*," said Erin with her exaggerated facial movements again.

"And I bet he has a huge cock," said Lo, unabashed.

"Don't go stereotyping," rebuked Val, "just cause he's black."

"I'm not stereotyping," said Lo, "anyone can see it when he wears that bathing suit."

The girls all laughed because they all knew that they had been looking and seeing exactly what Lo was talking about.

Kaylee laughed too and said, "Yeah, I am lucky that way. Even if it's boring, it *is massive*. The first time I slept with him I thought I was going to *die*. No, really – I couldn't take all that ... length and girth. I thought he was splitting me in two. I had to beg him to stop."

Lo looked at me and I at her because I know that that is exactly what she longs for. I mean, I'm well-endowed and thankful for every inch of it, but Lo has had larger, and her holy grail is a cock she can't accommodate.

The girls laughed and giggled, and this caught the attention of the guys by the grill. One of them called out, "What's so funny over there?" This threw the girls into hysterics. The guys ignored them as silly and Kaylee went on: "So, I can't complain, but it would be nice if he used some of those muscles on me in some other ways."

"Then you *have* to read this book," said Val, "and never mind that it was your mom who recommended it to you."

"Or," said Lo, "have Cory read it to you and see if you don't both find something you're comfortable with."

Bathsheba at the Beach

During this confidential chat about sex – a chat that I imagine many cliques of women had that summer due to the unprecedented explosion of this "Mommy Porn" series – the guys – Jeff, Dan, Steve, and Cory – were all having relaxed banter with Sally by the grill. If I am to be polite, I should introduce you, dear reader, to Sally. In many ways Sally is Lo's nemesis: a blond, flirtatious floozy, a former cheerleader, who is a glutton for attention. Lo has always had a bit of a rivalry with Sally and, during an unguarded moment, would descry Sally as a fraud, a charlatan, an imposter. "She pretends to be a slut," she once said to me, "but I'm the real thing, the genuine article. I hate her ostentatious flaunting of her tits and ass. I, on the other hand, can't keep my hands off my own assets, let alone anyone else's."

Sally was dating Jeff, a tall, lanky fella who always reminded me a bit of a country bumpkin. He spoke slowly and he was not particularly interesting. He observed Sally's behavior with quiet reservation, and I often wondered what he thought of her and what she saw in him. I don't know what the guys and Sally were talking about, but I could see, from my occasional glances over their way, that Sally was holding the rapt attention of the men. She wore a tiny little red bikini that looked two sizes too small for her on top, causing a lot of cleavage, and three sizes too small on the bottom, revealing a lot of her butt.

When she overheard the laughter from our area, or perhaps saw the girls talking in hushed tones, she grew curious and drew up a lounge chair by us.

"What are you girls gossiping about?" she asked, eager to know. I was glad to be included in her "girls."

"*Fifty Shades of Grey*," one of the girls responded.

"Oh," she said, smiling. "It's overrated," she pronounced, as if her word was the objective truth on the subject.

I could see that this upset Lo, not only because it was identical with Lo's opinion of the book, but because Sally had the audacity to say it in just that tone; a dismissive tone that Lo likes to use when talking about restaurants she no longer frequents. Often the people who are most like us are the ones who most aggravate us. That was the case here. And, as if Sally's words weren't enough, what she did next really caused Lo to steam. Since we were on the beach during the off season, there were no lifeguards and few other vacationers. Taking full advantage of this relative privacy, Sally undid her bikini top and said that she sees no reason for tan lines.

When Lo saw this, she was not about to be outdone by that little wench. Immediately Lo removed her top, with a carefully constructed smile, and said she completely agreed. Lo looked at me in a threatening fashion implying that I had better only have eyes for her rack and *not* Sally's. But, the other three ladies followed suit, one by one, either with caution and modesty or care-free, till all five of them were proudly displaying their chests.

The guys then announced that the burgers and steaks were done, and we all got up and sat over by the outdoor table, each grabbing plates and various condiments for lunch. After a few minutes of sitting together eating and trying to make small talk, the toplessness of the ladies became awkward and uncomfortable and so they either put their tops back on or put on t-shirts. Lo grabbed her white see-through top and happily enjoyed her meal. Val, though, remained unabashedly topless as Ruggles came over to the table to beg for scraps.

After lunch, Lo and I went for a long walk along the shore and talked about her weekend so far. Most of what she had to say was about Sally and how she had really had just about all she could stand of "that whore" this weekend. I laughed and joked with Lo, saying that she's only angry at Sally because she's stealing all of her own tricks. "Yeah, so?! What of it?" said Lo, aware that her ire was irrational. "You know," she went on, "that she only pulled that 'tan lines' bullshit stunt to grab your attention."

"Now Lo, I don't really think that ..."

Before I could finish, Lo interrupted, saying, "Of course she did! You can't possibly believe that she's happy with that dolt, Jeff, can you? No, she wants someone like you – older, stronger, well built, a silver fox."

I admit, though I didn't believe Lo, it was nice to hear. "Go on," I said, letting my vanity get the best of me.

Lo pushed me down into the sand and got on top of me, "Daddy, I want you so bad!"

"Lo, you're going to have to wait. This is not the time, nor the place for this."

She rocked back and forth on my cock and made sure to make it good and hard before relenting and letting me up. My tent pole was up, and the tent of my suit draped around it. How terribly embarrassing. There was nothing to do but run into the cool waves of the ocean. Lo followed. We swam for a while and Lo kept going underwater and taking my cock in her mouth.

"Lo," I said when she came up for air, "if you're a good girl and wait, I'll make it worth your while. Believe me, I want you as badly as you want me."

We swam back to our crew and now most of them were up on the deck drinking. I went up to grab a cold beer, but Lo said she was going to shower first. "You'll watch me, right Daddy?"

She went into the outdoor shower she had told me about the previous day, and I went up on the deck, but before I could get to the side to watch my little Lo bathing below me, like Bathsheba before David, I was intercepted by Jeff. He began with some small talk and offering me a beer. Of course, I appreciated the cold one on the hot day, but I wished to do nothing more than bypass the chit-chat and view my lovely bathing beauty. I was practically standing on tiptoes trying to gain some perspective on the action below without arousing suspicion or attention. Jeff went on about his work, sports, and money – all subjects I couldn't give a farthing about. Finally, parched from all his talking (or so I assumed) he said his beer was empty and he was going to get another. Not a moment too soon!

I saw Lo's hat protecting her lovely head from the sun like a sombrero as she sat on the small bench and removed her bathing suit. Then she removed the hat as well, tuning on the water and testing its temperature. I was practically falling off the railing when suddenly there was a slap on my back. It was Jeff again. Apparently, he's fond of me.

"What ya loo..." Before he could get out the whole question, he saw what I was looking at. Yes. My Lo. Naked. Under the shower. Did I mention, naked? Lathering up. Washing down. Rubbing. Pinching. Fondling. And then, as the two of us stared in silence, she grabbed the shampoo bottle and placed it on the bench, pulled her knees up under her on the bench, and slowly, gradually, descended upon the bottle – swallowing it with her pussy lips. One hand spread her pussy, the other rubbed her clit furiously as she enveloped the thick cylinder all the way down to the base.

"Hey ..." Jeff began to call to the others, but I grabbed his arm and gave him a serious look, implying that he'd better shut his pie hole if he knows what's good for him and just enjoy the show. He looked back at me as understanding slowly rippled over his face. He turned again to Lo and said to me in a more confidential tone, "How do you put up with it, H.? I mean, Sally is always flirting – you know that – and it drives me crazy. Like today when she took off her top in front of you and everyone else. But you, you seem to take it all in stride. I mean, just look at her. She's a fucking fuck-crazy whore."

"Is that what you really think of my girlfriend?" I asked, toying with him, cruelly.

"Sorry," he said, "but you should have seen her this week."

"What do you mean?" I inquired, keeping my eyes fixed on my Bathsheba below.

"You know how this house is laid out. And you know where Lo's room is. Every night we might be sitting around watching TV or drinking in the living room or kitchen and she'd announce at some point that she was getting tired and that we were in her bedroom. She'd then get undressed right down to her thong. She'd throw over a t-shirt or something and hop in the pullout bed and say we're welcome to stick around. Different people would be in bed with her on different nights and, I swear to you, I'm pretty sure that while we were watching TV or what have you, she was sitting there touching herself under the covers."

Yep, that sounded like my Lo – reverting to her college-days ways.

"But last night," he went on, "we were up drinking late, and the same routine happened, but this time Sally got in bed with Lo. I was over by the kitchen and others were in the chairs in the living room and we were watching a movie. I wasn't paying too much attention to Lo and Sally – hoping Sally wouldn't make a scene, drawing attention to herself like she always does. But as soon as the movie was over, Sally turned on some porn channel. Before long, Sally and Lo were making out. The guys were all encouraging them and egging them on, and then Sally went below the sheets and went down on Lo who came and came hard in front of everyone. The guys applauded and laughed like it was a big joke, but I was furious at Sally, who then appeared from under the sheets with a giant grin on her face."

Meanwhile, as Jeff was telling me this, Lo was furiously pumping up and down on that shampoo bottle – her tits bouncing, her eyes shut, her mouth open, water streaming down her glistening body in the sun, and – I wouldn't be surprised – her pussy squirting all over that thing. I managed to take my eyes off Lo for a moment to look at Jeff and I had a realization; Jeff is my antipode, just as Sally is Lo's. Or, maybe, he is just the person I used to be thirty years ago.

I looked back at my Lo, as did Jeff, and I said slowly, "Jeff, you know, I don't begrudge Lola any pleasure she may seek out and take because there she is, a young woman in the throes of her sexuality, full of life, love, lust, and libido. And here I am, a middle-aged man, wildly devoted to her, madly in love with her, but, between you and me, unable to keep up with her sexually. Love, Jeff, is about wanting the good of your partner for your partner, not wanting your partner's goods all to yourself. I want Lo to be happy. If that means doing things like this, then that's ok by me."

"But aren't you ..." he considered his words carefully, "*embarrassed* by her?"

"Embarrassed? Embarrassed, how?"

"I mean," he looked down at Lo, whose galloping motions were now slowing to a canter, "she's such a," and again he tried to find a delicate word and failed, "such a slut."

Oh, the poor boy. Caught, still, in the slut/stud, sinner/saint, virgin/whore dichotomy that has plagued Western sexuality since Eve and Lilith and only became worse with the whole cult of the Virgin that blossomed in the 12th Century.

I couldn't help but let out a little laugh. "Jeff," I said, "you're never going to be happy with Sally or any woman until you learn that love is not limited or limiting. Love is license. Love is liberating. Love is the levity of life. I've often wondered why the idiom is 'falling in love.' Why *falling*? So passive. Why not *leaping*? Leaping into love. Leaping up to love. It is an elevated, ecstatic experience, not a tumble down. Remember, my friend, the immortal words of Blake when he said, 'He who binds to himself a joy does the winged life destroy, but he who kisses the joy as it flies lives in eternity's sunrise.' Would you believe me if I told you that for all her whoring around, just about every night Lo begs me to put her collar around her neck, place her on a leash, and walk her about the house as if she were my dog? Would you believe me if I told you that she constantly implores me to 'mark my territory,' as she calls it, by cumming in her and through other physical acts? Would you believe me if I told you that every night, she calls me 'Sir,' and 'Master,' and repeatedly professes her devotion to me? Jeff, my friend, I pity you and the pain you must be going through. I was there myself once. But it wasn't until I found true love – a leaping, unbounded, unlimited love – that I realized how foolish I had been. Even so, Lo doesn't quite comprehend these mysteries herself. She still strives to make me jealous, get me to punish her for her indiscretions, show her that she's mine. But, deep down, I truly believe that she does get it and that these little protestations of hers are all part of the game."

Prospero & Miranda

I looked down at my Bathsheba bathing naked in the outdoor shower and saw her dismounting from her shampoo bottle. She spread her legs and allowed the hot water to rush over her stretched and abused pussy, massaging it tenderly. She looked up at me and Jeff and blew me a kiss. She rinsed out her bathing suit and put it back on, and soon she was up on the deck with the rest of us. She was walking gingerly and her enlarged pussy lips were *very* visible through the white bikini bottoms, but other than that, she was radiant and looked completely refreshed. She came up to me and Jeff and I said, "Good shower, dear?"

"Oh, you have no idea," she said, kissing me, but looking at Jeff. "What have you two been up to?" she asked, as she looked down at the rock-solid hard-ons in our bathing suits.

"We're just talking."

"About what?"

"Relationships and their complexities."

"Oh, well, I don't think relationships are complex at all. You just give me what I want and we're both happy. Simple," she said as her right hand reached down to stroke my cock over my shorts. "I think I'm going to go take a nap. Come with me." She meant that in both senses of the word. She gave me a sidelong glance as she walked away and went into the house. I followed her into the living room. She pulled out the bed and lay down on it. She removed her bathing suit, dried herself off with a towel, and got under the covers.

"Come on, Daddy. I know you want to."

"Lo! No. Not here. Not now."

"Don't you want it, Daddy?" she asked as she pulled the sheets back and rubbed her already red, sore, and swollen pussy.

"Of course, I want it after that show you put on in the shower," I exclaimed, "but I'm not going to fuck you right here."

"Oh, you don't have to fuck me, Daddy, just lie down with me."

"Oh no, Lo, I'm not going to fall for that. I know exactly what you're up to. I know your little games. I am *not* lying down."

"Oh, please, Daddy," she said as she got on all fours like a dog and looked up at me. "You can even have my ass." She pivoted around so that her ass was now facing me and she was fingering it slowly.

"Lo, everyone can see you. They can see us. They could walk in here at any moment to grab a beer or a sandwich."

"Oh fiddle-dee-dee," she said.

"I'm leaving this very minute."

"No, Daddy, don't! Please. I'll be good."

I stood there waiting for evidence of her goodness.

"Just tell me something, Daddy," she asked, "how much do you want me?"

"Lo, I can't even begin to tell you how much I want you."

"A lot?"

"A very lot!"

"Good."

"Is that all?"

"Yes, Daddy."

"OK, then. I'm going back outside."

"But Daddy, I'm *so* wet still."

"Lo! Put those sheets over yourself."

"Yes, Daddy. But tonight – you promise?"

"Yes, I promise."

I turned and walked outside. I'm not sure what Lo was up to inside. Under normal circumstances I would guess that she was jillin' it, but after what she just did to herself in the shower, I doubted that she was capable of it, no matter how much she wanted to.

I joined everyone else who was sitting at the long table beside the grill and grabbed another beer.

"Where's Lo?" someone asked.

"Napping, I think," I answered.

This reply was met with smiles and grins by all.

"What?" I asked.

The guys and gals then proceeded to tell me that I must really be something special. The women said that they've never seen Lo like this. Not in college, not ever. By "this" they meant so overtly sexual. I heard a recounting of the Sally incident of the previous night and other scandalous stories. I looked at them and demurely said, "Well, I appreciate the compliment, but I assure you, it's not me. You know that 'sex' is Lo's chosen field and I just think that graduate school and her studies have brought out a less inhibited side of her."

The ladies giggled and the guys raised their eyebrows.

"H," one of them said, "all she speaks about is you. She's totally crazy about you. It's 'H.H. this and H.H. that.' You've definitely changed her. She's never been like this."

I think I must have begun to blush. Before I could find some response, Sally came over and sat on the picnic bench next to me. Or rather, she straddled it so that she was sitting perpendicular to me with her legs spread; her bikini bottom just barely concealing her crotch. "Tell us, H.H., about your writing."

Uh oh. What, I wondered, has Lo told them?

"What about my writing?" I asked, trying to get a sense of where this was going.

"You know," Sally said, "the blog?"

Yikes! She told them.

"What would you like to know?"

"How about ... the name of the blog," she said almost demandingly.

"Uh uh," I replied, shaking my head 'no.'

"OK, well, tell us what it's about."

"Sounds like Lo already told you," I said, trying to be coy.

"She told us it's a *sex blog*," she said, whispering the last two words with emphasis.

"It's a place where Lo and I can share our ... experiences."

"What experiences?"

"That's not for me to say. Whatever Lo wants to tell you, she can. But, other than that, I really can't go into detail."

"Please," Sally said, sliding her sexy legs closer to me so one of her knees was touching mine.

"Leave the guy alone," said Jeff in a tone of complaint.

"OK," said Sally, "but if it's out there, I'll find it."

She got up from her seat and ran her fingers up my side, over my shoulder and to my neck and hair. I felt incredibly uncomfortable, like I had done something wrong or unfaithful.

Not more than five minutes went by before my cell phone vibrated. I looked at it and saw a text from Lo: "Just came again."

Damn!

Fifteen minutes later she returned to my side and said, "I'm bored." Now she was wearing a pretty yellow bikini – too small on the top and bottom – that was very cute on her.

She sat down next to me. The dog, Ruggles, came up to us. Lo pet it, but the bitch was clearly vying for my attention. I ignored it.

"Oh look," said Lo to me, "she's just like me. She gets off on your indifference."

After an awkward moment of petting the dog on the head, I turned to Lo and asked, "What would you like to do, sweetheart?"

"Bumper boats!"

"What?"

"Bumper boats," she repeated with a nod of her head up and down.

So, that afternoon Lo and a carload of our friends went driving down the main vacation drag, and we not only rode the bumper boats, but did one round of go-cart racing, a round of mini-golf, and we topped off our child-like antics with some ice cream. Of course, after each indulgence of her whims, Lo grabbed my arm, lifted herself up to my ear, and whispered, "Thank you, Daddy," as I extended my hand to pay the fare.

We returned to the beach house and stoked the outdoor fire pit, grilled up some food on the BBQ, had dinner and drinks and sat around talking till the sun descended over the waves. It was an unusually warm night for September. It was one of those nights where it feels like tropical air is moving in from the shore. Lo suggested a midnight swim. Six of us walked down through the silent sand as the moonlight illuminated the crest of the waves causing them to shimmer silver when they broke. Lo whispered in my ear, "It would be romantic to skinny dip" and she pulled me off to the side where she removed my bathing suit and then enthusiastically took off hers.

We waded into the warm water a bit apart from the rest of the crew. After we got past the resistance of the waves crashing down on us, I held her in my arms as we gently floated up with the swelling waves and we were just as gently let down after they passed. When the arched back of the waves lifted us, we couldn't touch bottom, but when they released us, the water was only barely up to our waists.

We gradually floated out a little further and Lo was snuggled up right against me; her hard nipples rubbing against my chest. As we got deeper, I could stand and Lo wrapped her legs around mine, pressing her pussy up against my cock. We kissed open mouthed as the waves made their crescendos and decrescendos. "Fuck me, Daddy," she insisted. I entered right into her below the water line and she let out a little moan as I watched her mouth open in the moonlight; her teeth reflecting the pale blue glint of the night. I eased in and out of her again and again until she came and she whispered in my ear, "Cum inside me. Now." I obediently, willingly, readily did as commanded. When I pulled out of her, she reached down with her right hand and held my cock firmly, enjoying its last gasp of girth.

We swam a bit more and rejoined our friends. We stayed under the dark water where they couldn't see that we were naked, though

I'm sure they must have suspected as much. Before long we all were getting out. Lo and I swam back to the area where we had gotten into the water, or so we thought, but we couldn't find our bathing suits. Had the tide come in and swallowed them up? We paced back and forth, naked in the moonlight, looking for our suits. They were nowhere to be found. There was nothing to do but to make our way back to the house where everyone was now on the deck by the fire. As we walked up like Prospero and Miranda, shipwrecked and naked, we explained what happened as we grabbed a couple of towels. We were roundly laughed at, jeered at, and were the butt of some jokes, but all in good fun.

We had a few more beers and talked till about midnight. The next day, Saturday, was the end of our vacation and everyone was feeling a bit tired out by now from all the sun, sea, and late nights. We all turned in rather early and when Lo and I got into our pull-out couch after everyone else had shut their doors, Lo whispered to me, "Fuck me again, Daddy."

Closet Exhibitionist

When Lo and I got into our pull-out couch after everyone else had shut their doors, Lo whispered to me, "Fuck me again, Daddy."

"Lo," I sighed, "I just fucked you."

"Do it again."

"Lo," I said in a tone that pleaded for mercy.

"Come on, Daddy-O" she said in a tone that pleaded for pleasure.

"No, really Lo, I can't."

"Oh, pooh!" she said dismissively, "You're a musket!"

"Yes, Lo, I'm a musket. One good shot is all you get out of me."

I rolled over on my back and I could hear her slapping her pussy in the dark.

I was almost asleep when she got up. To my surprise she put on a tee shirt and panties. What the hell was she doing? "Going somewhere?" I asked.

"You're snoring. I can't sleep."

"Where are you going?"

"I don't know yet. In one of the bedrooms."

There were four doors off the living room. It was like a gameshow. Which door would Lo pick: Jeff and Sally, Kaylee and Cory, Val and Dan, or Steve and Erin? She went from one to the other in indecision. And then she finally picked one, knocked lightly, and went in. I didn't even know whose it was until the next day when she told me the story of her nocturnal activities.

But, before I get to retelling the tale I heard from Lo, I would be remiss if I didn't inform you about the odd game of musical beds that happened that night. Moments after Lo got up from our pullout couch and chose the prize behind door number four, Erin appeared, walking through the living room, ostensibly to get a glass of water from the fridge in the kitchen. She was wearing only a long pink t-shirt, barely covering her pink panty-clad butt. As she began tiptoeing through the living room, she looked over at me and saw me sitting by the small lamp on the bed reading a book with the covers draped over my legs.

"Where's Lo?" she whispered, looking around the room.

I was in a real predicament. What do I say? Do I lie and say she's in the bathroom or she went for a walk, or do I tell her that she got up out of sexual frustration with me and went into one of the bedrooms on the prowl for something to feed her hungry pussy? Unable to formulate any response, I just shrugged my shoulders stupidly.

She grabbed her water bottle from the fridge and sat down on the bed next to me. "Are you ok?"

"Yeah, why?"

"I don't know. There's something in your eyes that just looks ... sad."

"No, Erin, I'm fine. Just reading. I am a bit tired from all the ... festivities." The truth was, having just cum in Lo, I was experiencing post-coital comatosis; my own term for the glazed look that ices over my face and the wave of exhaustion I feel whenever I ejaculate. Lo hates it because the reaction she has to orgasm (hers or mine) is a desire for another. So, when I have climaxed, it is nothing short of coitus interruptus for her when I lie on my back or grab a pillow, turn over, and fall into a deep sleep. That's why I so frequently attempt to prevent my own climax or have what I refer to as an "internal orgasm." This is the sensation of orgasm experienced by a man without actual ejaculation. I thought I had discovered it myself, but it turns out it is an ancient practice, perfected by tantric yoga techniques.

"Are you ok?" I asked her as I awkwardly grasped for something to fill the silence.

"Oh yeah," she said, "just thirsty." She took a sip of her water, but looked into my eyes as she did so. It got even more awkward. Then she said, "I don't get it."

"Get what?" I inquired.

"You know."

"What? I don't know."

"I don't get ... you and Lo."

"What do you mean?"

She was clearly growing slightly frustrated with my lack of comprehension, but I honestly had no idea where she was going with this.

"I'm sorry, it's really none of my business," she said, "but ..." She trailed off, trying to think how to best put it. "But you're such a nice guy and ..." Again, she trailed off. "Don't get me wrong, Lo is one of my best friends, but ... I guess it's cause we are such good friends that she has told me, she's told me about your 'open relationship.'" As she said the words, her face made that exaggerated expression, and she practically whispered the phrase as if it were a crime. "And she's told all of us about the blog you two have, but she refuses to tell us how we can see it for ourselves. But I just don't get it," she repeated again, as if it were a math problem that she had to figure out or she'd fail.

"What part don't you get?" I asked, as if I were the math instructor, trying to break it down for her.

"Pretty much all of it. I mean, her having sex with other guys – it sort of implies that you're not enough for her; that you're not enough of a man. Doesn't it upset you?"

A smile came across my face. She really was totally in the dark about our relationship.

"No, it doesn't upset me at all. I encourage it."

"What?"

"I encourage it. Look, I love Lo. I love her completely and faithfully. I want whatever it is she wants. And, well, if you're such a good friend of Lo's, you must know that she wants a *lot* of sex."

"I get that impression," she said sarcastically.

"Her demand outstrips my supply, let's say. I'm twice her age. I get all I want, all I need, all I can handle, and then some."

"But in every relationship, there are discrepancies between the partners' needs. I mean sexually. People just deal with it."

"The other part of it is, it turns me on to see Lo with other guys, and with other women too, though she usually keeps those relationships more private."

"*That* I just don't get."

"It's a kink. It's a thing. It's called 'cuckolding' and there are a lot of people who are into it. Look it up some time." I was a bit resentful, a bit angry, a bit embarrassed to have to say this to Erin. I mean, if a "normal" heterosexual couple is into dirty talk, or if they have a particular kink about foot massages, or whatever, no one ever calls them out on it and forces them to explain. Now I understand that with Lo and me it's different. First, Lo apparently raised the topic with her friends, and so it is a legitimate discussion to have, just as if, had Erin mentioned that she liked foot massages and she got off from that, we could inquire about it. But if she was aroused by foot massages and I wasn't, would I judge her? No. Would I press the issue as if she were a freak? No. Would I continue to ask probing questions to try and 'get' why she liked it so much? No. I might try it myself, but I wouldn't hold her responsible for engaging in some morally indefensible conduct.

"It doesn't *bother* you? You don't get *jealous*?" Now her face was contorting all the way down her neck with the emphasis she was placing on the words.

"No, not in the least. I know Lo loves me. She professes it night and day. I've *never* been with any woman who has been so in love with me, said it so frequently, expressed it in so many ways, and with whom I felt I could trust her 100 percent."

"How can you trust her 100 percent when she's sleeping with other people?"

"I trust that she only wants what is best for me and for our relationship. If I said today that her sexploits bothered me, I know she'd stop in a heartbeat. But then I would have to face the full brunt of her libido without any help."

At that very moment, a low moan (or a 'Lo moan') escaped from behind one of the doors. Both Erin and I stopped to listen for a moment, but there were no follow-up noises.

"That doesn't bother you?" she asked as her eyes scanned the doors around us, trying to figure out which room Lo was in.

"Believe it or not, whatever is going on in there will bring us closer together later. It's just fuel for the fire of our relationship."

"Material for the blog?"

"Yeah, that too."

"It's one thing to like to watch Lo with other guys, but why do you have to publish it for everyone to see?"

I was losing patience with Erin at this point. The chasm between her puny Puritanical bandwidth and our broadminded, progressive lifestyle seemed beyond bridging. But, having nothing better to do at the time, except for listening in on Lo's *ménage à trois*, I humored her questions. I said, "A few years back I had a best female friend with whom I e-mailed just about daily, and I shared with her lots of intimate stuff. It was like journaling, but with a sounding board, a sympathetic listener. But then stuff happened, she and I drifted apart, a rift in the relationship occurred, and we grew further from one another rather than closer. At the same time, things unfolded with Lo and there was no one I knew in whom I could confide. I mean, Lo totally blew my mind and continues to do so. I needed an outlet for all that was happening in my life; someone to talk to about it. Even if I could confide in a friend, who would believe me, really? I went on-line to look for other guys who were dating nymphomaniacs – I mean, that is what Lo is, you know. I hope that's not too much info for you. Anyhow, I searched and searched and couldn't find hardly anyone who was in my same situation. I was hoping to find a blog or a website about it, but there was nothing. So, I took matters in my own hand and began writing about my sex life with Lola. About a month or so into my blogging, I realized, 'Wow! This has taken the place of my e-mail correspondence. But it's so much better since I get a variety of views and not just one in return.' That was the original reason for blogging on my part. But for Lo, well, let's just say she's not only a nympho, but also a bit of a closet exhibitionist. I realize that's an oxymoron, but that's really what she is. She doesn't let on too frequently in public how much she likes the attention (around you and her other close friends, it's different), but she loves to get naked for the camera and put on a real show. It turns her on even more when I post pornographic pics of her on the blog, and we get all sorts of fan mail from readers. They tell us about how much they enjoy the stories about her nymphomaniac hijinks and that they really got off to her pics. That really gets her riled up and me too. Cause, for me, it's like dating a porn star."

Erin shriveled up her face and let out an "Ewwwww," as she then mimed a gag reflex. Apparently, the thought of strange guys out there (who knows where?) masturbating to photos of her dear friend was not as welcome a thought to Erin as it is to Lo. Little does she know that most of our fans turn out to be women; I wonder if Erin has any clue as to how frequently those women tell us about jillin' it to our blog?

In any case, I could see that, far from making headway in explaining why we do what we do, I was merely creating more confusion and repulsion in the mind of my late-night companion. Rather than approach me with an open mind and genuine curiosity about the topic, it was becoming increasingly clear to me that Erin just asked so that she could confirm her already fully formed negative judgment of our arrangement.

"Erin," I said, "I'm not asking you to approve what we do. Frankly, I don't care what you think. I'm not trying to convince you to try it or do it or practice it. If whatever you and Steve do makes you happy, if it works for you, then great! Go for it! All I'm trying to do is answer your question and explain what you apparently don't 'get': why I'm with Lo and why she makes me happy. But to be very, very honest with you, I pour my heart and soul into the writing I do on the blog. The blog is really the place where I try to tell whoever will listen exactly why I love Lo so much. I mean, yes, a lot of it does have to do with her nymphomaniac tendencies, her autoerotic behaviors, her exhibitionist qualities, her incredibly hot and steamy sex (with me and others), but that's only part of the story. To get it all, you'd have to read the whole blog. And even then, whatever it is that sends those sparks flying between us – that magical flame that burns in each of us for the other – capturing that in words is just as impossible as grabbing hold of fire with your hands. If you want to 'get it,' then read the blog. Maybe that would help you understand."

"Even if I could," Erin said, almost apologetically, "Lo won't tell me how to find it. She's so secretive about it."

"Well, of course she is. She doesn't want her best friends seeing that!"

"But it's fine for strangers to ogle it?"

"That's her prerogative, I guess. But I totally understand how she feels. I mean, I'm happy to tell the world about my sex life with Lola, but I wouldn't want my friends reading it either. You just don't want them knowing your deepest, most intimate moments. It's paradoxical, but it makes sense ... to me, anyhow."

"So, you're not going to tell me?"

Something about that question just struck me as odd. Did she *want* to read it? But she just turned her nose up at it. Why did she want to read it? Did she have ulterior motives? Did she have a latent freak-flag just bursting to be unfurled? Did she need to be inspired by Lo? Her interest was suspicious. But I did enjoy the joke of telling her exactly where she could find the blog – twice – without her realizing it. I hid it right in plain sight.

I looked at her and said, "Erin, if it were only up to me, I'd be happy for you to read it. I'd tell you in a heartbeat where to find it. I'd be honored if you read it. But it's not my place to out Lo. If you want to read it, you'll have to ask her yourself."

Erin was about to say something when we both heard a very audible moan from behind one of the closed doors again.

We looked at each other for a while, until it got uncomfortable, and then she said goodnight. I continued reading for a bit, fixed myself a whiskey, and by the time I was done drinking it, my eyes were no longer able to stay open.

The next thing I knew there was an incredibly bright light in the room and some movement around me. I had no idea where I was, but it turned out I was right where I had fallen asleep. The morning sun pierced the sliding glass doors of the living room like a beacon. Val and Dan were up and about. They had just taken Ruggles for a long walk on the beach and they were making breakfast. I'm usually up with the sun, but all of this – the light, the sounds, the movement, the people – was happening far too early for me. I tried to bury my head in the pillows, but to no avail. I couldn't sleep knowing that people were going about their day around me.

I got up and Val, in her usual chipper way, greeted me with a "Good morning!" She was practically giggling, but that's just the way she is always. Then she said the most wonderful five words I could have heard that morning: "Would you like some coffee?" Oh yes, yes I would. She poured me a mug full, and I went out on the deck to watch the sun rise over the ocean and see the various people out for jogs and walks on the shore.

I thought about my conversation with Erin the previous night. I thought of how odd her questions were; how rude, really. How curious that she wanted to read the blog. I thought of how funny it would have been if Lo had entered her room and she had come out to talk with me (or perhaps seduce me) while Lo was in the bedroom with her Steve. But I felt fairly certain that that wasn't the case. I wondered which couple Lo had ultimately shacked up with. If it wasn't Erin and Steve and it wasn't, apparently, Dan and Val (unless Lo was still deep in sleep in their room), then it was either Sally and Jeff or Kaylee and Cory. It was a tossup between either couple. Lo seemed to have some sort of love/hate relationship with Sally over the weekend. Of the two couples, she probably had better chances being welcome into their bed. But Lo lusts after large cock and so, based upon the previous day's conversation, she may have gravitated to Kaylee and Cory.

The Aesthete & The Slut

As I sat on the deck watching the morning unfold on the beach, I felt two warm arms wrap around me – flesh my flesh instantly identified as Lo's. (We have a carnal knowledge of each other as if the molecules of her body and the molecules of mine are in a symbiotic magnetic field of attraction to one another – something I suppose a more prosaic writer would call "animal magnetism.")

"Morning, Daddy," she whispered in my ear, inserting her tongue – an unexpected penetration of my auditory orifice that caused the hairs on the back of my neck to stand on end. She then kissed me down my neck and swung around to sit on my lap, almost spilling my coffee.

"Well, well, if it isn't my little night crawler."

"Oh, Daddy, don't be cross with me," she said as she kissed me on the lips. She was wearing nothing but an oversized t-shirt – not hers and not mine.

I scrunched up my face in a mock look of disgust and said, "I hate to think where those lips have been in the past ten hours."

"Oh shut up, Daddy-O," she said dismissively, "you know you can't wait to find out."

She kissed me again and reached down between my legs to grab my cock.

"Oh, Daddy," she said in a deep sigh, dropping her head back, "I want it."

"Lo!"

"Just pull my nipples."

"Really Lo," I said in shock.

"Just one pinch. Please."

I did as she asked. She pulled away. "Ow," she said, "I'm *so* sore from last night."

Damn! I fell right into her little trap.

"OK, I'll bite," I said, "What happened last night?"

"You'll just have to wait till later to hear that story, Daddy," she said in her teasing tone.

"Just tell me this much," I asked, "whose room did you go to?"

"Oh no, Daddy-O," she said as she began to get up from my lap, "I need a cup of coffee before we talk about anything." She started to walk away, but I pulled her by her arm so that she was bending over me, looking me right in the eyes. The position she was in caused her t-shirt to slip up, revealing a bit – a cute bit – of her rear. "Lo," I said, seriously, "you're driving me crazy."

"Me?" she said innocently, "I'm driving *you* crazy? Oh, old man, you have no idea how you drive *me* crazy." As she said this, she reached down again to grab my balls. She looked down between my legs. Hungrily, her mouth opened to say something, but before she could utter a word, Cory came up from behind Lo and grabbed her ass cheek with his big hand. He squeezed hard as he said, "H.H., you really got a nice piece of ass here."

Lo stood straight up, and without a moment's thought, turned and slapped him across the face. She then walked into the house, turning to blow a kiss at me. She stopped at the door and said, "You want me to warm up your mug?"

Both Cory and I were stunned and perplexed. I said, "Uh, no, no thanks."

"OK," said Lo as she turned 'round, pulling up the hem of her t-shirt to flash us a quick peek of her red butt before she disappeared inside the sliding door.

"Wow!" said Cory, rubbing his face where Lo had slapped him. "What is *with* that girl?!"

"You, Kaylee, and Lo had a good night, I trust?"

He pulled up a chair and sat down and said, "H.H., you're one lucky guy or one unlucky son-of-a-bitch. I don't know which, but I guess it depends upon how *you* think about it. I'll tell you this much; last night is a night I won't soon forget."

To be honest with you, I really didn't want to hear anything about last night from him before I heard it from Lo. But, there I was and all I could do is sit there and be polite. To make matters worse, he grabbed a chair and was sitting in front of me, shirtless, wearing only his blue boxers with a perfectly defined profile of his endowment hanging in front of me, as if to throw in my face what Lo enjoyed last night.

His wide grin was there in front of me, shining like the white sand in the bright morning sun, and I had nothing to reply at the moment, so I sat mutely until Lo returned with her coffee. She sat on my lap again and asked, "Did you sleep well?" I felt as if she was mocking me, but I replied with, "Oh yeah, once I was able to get Erin out of my bed."

"Erin! What was Erin doing in your bed?"

"I guess you'll just have to wait to hear that story, won't ya?"

She got up from my lap and sat on Cory's lap and said, "Do you see how mean he is to me?"

Cory laughed and then Kaylee walked in, wearing cute pink sweats that said "PINK" over her ass and a tank top. "Get off my boyfriend, you slut!" she said in a joking tone.

Lo looked up at her and said, "Oh, come on, there's enough here for us to share." Lo made the motion with her tongue licking her lips as she looked down at Cory's protruding penis.

Both girls laughed and then Lo got up and said, "Oh, ok, I guess you can have him back. I'll sit with my sulking Steppenwolf." She came over to me and sat on my lap and said, "Don't worry, there's enough of me to share too." Kaylee sat on Cory's lap and the three of them passed the time making small talk about this and that as I held my baby-girl in my arms, lusting after her smooth flesh and caressing the soft skin of her knee.

Eventually we all got up and, though breakfast would have been nice, we had to rush because it was Saturday, our last day there, and we had to clean up and be out by noon. As we were working hard to get the place in order, Erin and Steve told all of us that they were having a little get-together at their apartment that night and we all could come by if we wanted to. It was a beginning of the school year party and there would be about 20 or so grad students coming by.

Lo and I contributed to cleaning up the mess the ten of us had made over the past few days and then, all tidied up, we left the key in the designated spot and hopped in our cars. Lo had driven out there with Val and Dan, but for the return trip, she'd be with me. We made a stop for a soft-serve (with a cherry of course) for Lo and then we took one more walk along the beach before getting on the road.

Leaving on a Saturday and after peak season, the ride was nice and simple. No traffic jams. No hot sun beating down on the black pavement. Just smooth sailing along the two-lane highway westward.

Lo was wearing her bikini (and still lamenting the loss of her yellow bikini to the thieving sea) and she began rubbing between her legs as we drove.

"OK, I'll bite," I said, "What happened last night?"

"Oh, Daddy, I thought you'd never ask."

"Yeah, yeah, sweetheart, let's cut to the chase. Give me the down and dirty."

"Well, after you wouldn't get it up for me, I decided to join Cory and Kaylee."

"I *knew* it!" I exclaimed. "I knew you would lust after that long cock."

"Oh, Daddy, don't be so pedestrian. It wasn't the cock I was longing for, so much as the pussy."

"What?!"

"That's right. You heard me. I wanted Kaylee's pretty pink cunt."

"Lo!" I said, feigning shock at her vulgarity and covering my right ear with my hand. "Come on," I continued, "you don't expect me to buy that for a minute, do you?"

"It's the truth. Kaylee and I had a brief fling together when we were in college."

"What?!" It's not that it was so difficult to believe that Lo would fool around with her good friend Kaylee, but that she hadn't revealed this interesting little bit of history to me prior to this surprised me.

"We were both sophomores and, well, we were both experimenting. She came over my dorm room and in short order I had her bent over and I was on my knees behind her using my tongue on her sweetly shaved pussy and ass."

Lo was really rubbing now, and she stuffed her right hand down her bikini bottom.

"Go on," I said, calmly.

"It was only a couple of night stands, but it was very fun, very exciting. She and I were both inexperienced with women and I liked exploring with her. So, when I couldn't get any from you, I thought I'd try to rekindle that old flame."

"I see," I said in a way that encouraged her to continue.

"I knocked gently," she said, "and then opened the door a crack."

As we drove on the winding highway, she told me the following story:

'Is it ok if I come in?' I asked. "H.H. is snoring and he took up the whole bed."

'Come on in,' said Kaylee. She was on the left side of the bed and Cory was on the right. I slid under the sheets next to her. She was in a t-shirt and her panties. Cory was next to her and I didn't know what he was wearing.

'He's so annoying,' I said about you. 'He spreads out like a bear, and I get a tiny sliver of the edge. Do you mind if I sleep here? I mean, I could go somewhere else if it's a problem.'

'No, it's fine,' said Kaylee.

'You're sure?'

'Sure.'

She rolled onto her side and put her left arm around me. She whispered in my ear so that Cory couldn't hear, 'I was hoping you'd come in.'

She licked or kissed my ear almost imperceptibly and then said, 'Remember that night ...?' She didn't even have to finish her question. I turned my face to hers and we kissed long kisses like we did that night in college. We both were feeling frisky, and we weren't quiet about it. Cory turned to hold Kaylee from behind and then he slowly entered her as she continued to kiss me and feel my breasts. She moaned, reached behind her to guide him in and then reached up under my shirt and lifted it over my hard nipples so she could suck and nibble at them. She was getting it good, long, and hard from Cory. She whispered in my ear, 'Cory is off limits. K?'

'No worries,' I heard Cory whisper, 'Nothing's gonna happen.'

I turned on my back and put my hand down my panties and began stroking my clit as she licked my neck and earlobe. Her left hand was pulling at my nipples. My back arched and bowed toward her fingertips as they pulled upward. My thighs were dripping. Her hand eventually moved slowly down my tum and further to feel my hands between my legs. She pulled my hands out and felt how I had soaked through my panties. She took over down below and I was cumming and cumming hard within seconds. I tried to stifle my moans, but could only grab a pillow with one hand and put it over my face.

At this point in her tale, Lo began cumming in the car – her hands furiously patting and slapping her pussy as we drove on at 60 miles an hour. She was screaming out as if she were making up for having to hold it in last night. It was a real struggle for me to keep my eyes on the road. My cock was as hard as the stick shift and I was unconsciously accelerating. When Lo finished, her hands instinctively reached over to my lap and felt my cock beneath my pants. She frantically pulled at the button and unzipped them and stretched over the console and put her mouth over my cock. My right hand held her head in place as I did my best to drive with my left. My eyes kept rolling to the back of my head of their own volition and my right foot kept on pressing the gas further and further down. I was about to cum when I saw that we had just passed a cop on the side of the road. Fuck! Was he going to go after me?

Yes. Yes he was.

I pulled over dutifully as I pulled Lo off my cock. She sat straight up in her seat and tried to straighten out her bikini. Meanwhile, my cock was still standing at attention, as if ready to salute the officer. Luckily, after he pulled us over, he took his own sweet time getting out of the cruiser. They like to do that, don't they? – Let you sit there and intimidate you with the stillness.

I put away my sergeant major and pulled out my license and registration. He sauntered over to the car with his super-trooper swagger. I looked up at him from the open window. He looked in the car and saw Lo's barely concealed body. He looked down at me.

"Do you know how fast you were going?"

"I believe I was going the speed limit, officer. I'm in no hurry."

"You were doing 80 in a 60 mile-an-hour zone."

"Oh, officer, I truly had no idea."

He scanned the car with his eyes – front seat, back seat, dash – looking for anything out of the ordinary.

"Can I see your ID, please," he said to Lo.

She had to turn and bend over the front seat, her little tush wiggling in the air, as she grabbed her beach bag in the back seat. I saw the officer watching this closely. His eyes followed the lines of her body from the front seat to the back and watched her breasts as they dangled in the air. Perv!

She grabbed her bag and sat back down in the front seat. She dug through the seemingly bottomless pit, pulling out her various items until she finally found her clutch. In it she took out a slew of cards, like she was getting ready to deal at poker, and finally she found her license. She leaned over me to give it to the officer as she batted her eyes at him, flashed a smile, and said, "Sorry for the delay officer."

He looked at it – no doubt checking the year of her birth.

He returned it to her and then asked us to wait while he walked slowly back to his cruiser to run my record.

I gave Lo a sidelong look.

"What?!" she exclaimed, as if innocent.

"You know what."

"Oh, Daddy." She grabbed my arm.

"You're a tease and he's a letch."

"What's that?" she asked with a twinkle in her eye, baiting me.

"You know how when we're driving in the car and an attractive woman crosses the street ..."

"You mean any woman in a short skirt?"

"Yeah, whatever. Anyhow, when you get upset, it's because you think I'm leering – you know, that's being a letch."

"So you're a letch?"

"No, I'm an aesthete."

"What's that?"

"A person who appreciates beauty in all its manifold manifestations."

"So, a letch. Just a pretentious letch."

While the lecherous cop was away, Lo put her arms around me and started kissing me. I had to physically push her back saying, "Lo, not the time or the time or the place!"

She pouted and sat in her seat while we awaited the return of the officer.

"I'm bored," she complained.

I was staring off at the horizon calculating what the fine was going to be.

After a good long time, he slowly but severely walked back to the driver's side window and handed me a ticket. ONE-HUNDRED DOLLARS! Damn it!

"Have a good day, ma'am," he said with a smile at Lo.

"Bye, officer," she said with a wink.

I waited for the chucklehead to drive away first and then I got back on the road.

Lo went back to rubbing her clit beneath her bikini bottoms and asked, "Don't you want to hear the rest of my story?"

"Grrrr," I grumbled.

I was agitated by so many things.

She leaned over and put her tongue in my ear. "Come on, Daddy. You have a hot woman in a bikini sitting in your passenger seat, putting her fingers down in her crotch, hot for you on a beautiful day with nothing between us but your dark cloud of gloom. Let some sun in there."

She began to run her tongue down my neck while I redoubled my efforts to concentrate on the road and keep my foot off the gas.

"Lo, sit down in your seat and calm it down till we get there."

"Oh pooh," she said, pouting, "Youth is wasted on the old!"

We drove a bit further and Lo pouted as I stewed in my anger about the ticket.

Suddenly she was slipping her bikini bottoms down over her thighs, around her knees, below her knees, around her ankles and off. "I'm really randy."

"Randy," I said, "I knew you were really a dude."

"What?"

"That's your real name, right?"

"Very funny," she said. "I only *wish* I were a dude. I wish I had a cock like that." She was massaging her very erect clit and looking over at my crotch as her tongue ran across her teeth and lips. "Oh," she moaned, "I'd love to have a cock like that."

"Lo, you already got me in trouble once with that!"

"But Daddy, I'm so hungry."

"I'm hungry too, Lo – we didn't have breakfast."

"I can skip breakfast, but I can't skip my morning masturbation."

She swiveled in her seat so that her legs were now up on the center console and her back to the door. She spread her legs and was rubbing her pussy. It took everything I had to stay focused.

"Get in the back seat and do that! I'm going to drive right off the road."

She climbed over the seat and hopped in the back. I could see her in the rear-view mirror. She sat on the edge of the seat and leaned forward so she was whispering in my ear as her right hand worked hard below my line of vision. She continued her story:

I lay on my back panting, heaving deep breaths trying to come back to myself. Cory was thrusting with his hips in and out of Kaylee. His big strong hands were reaching around her torso and grabbing her breasts. Her mouth was open, looking inviting. I turned my head to her and began kissing her. I reached my arms around her and rubbed my hands up and down Cory's curvaceous and hard biceps. I caressed him up to his shoulders. I was kissing her and feeling him. She held me and reached around to my ass. I spread my legs and held her body between my legs. I kept rubbing Cory's arms and I could hear his breathing growing heavier. I slid my mouth down Kaylee's neck down to her breasts. I kissed Cory's hands and nudged my lips in and on to her nipples. I sucked and nibbled. At some point I took Cory's large finger in my mouth and sucked on that as if it were his dick. Deep into the back of my throat I pushed it to let him know what I could take. Eventually though, I continued my downward descent, and I went to her navel and, under the covers, I kissed her pussy as Cory increased the speed with which he sawed away at her. I positioned my face right between Kaylee's legs and then, as if he knew *exactly* what I wanted, he pulled out of her pussy and put his cock right into my mouth and exploded in my mouth. Oh God! – it was big! Oh, oh!

She was cumming again in the back seat. She leaned back and eventually got horizontal on the seat and spread her legs – both hands working hard between her legs. "I'm squirting, Daddy!" I couldn't see anything. My poor fabric seats. Oh well.

Some time passed as all I could hear was deep breathing from the back seat. When it sounded like Lo's breathing had returned to normal, I asked her, "Wasn't Kaylee upset? I mean, she said specifically that you weren't to do anything with Cory."

"My mouth was full of his cum," said Lola, "and I swallowed it all, hungrily. I could taste her on his cock for a split second before he came. It was delicious!"

She climbed back into the front seat – still not wearing any bottoms – and pulled out of her bag some moisturizing cream. Putting her feet up on the dashboard, she began rubbing in the lotion slowly and seductively as she talked.

When I popped up above the covers, I kissed Kaylee and whispered in her ear, 'Oh my God, he's so fucking hot! I bet you and I could get him to try some kink on you.' It was clear that Kaylee hadn't cum yet and at this point I had already cum twice and Cory once. She was aching for a good orgasm. I whispered to her, 'Is he good for more than one?'

'Not usually,' she said.

'Let's see what we can do.'

I turned on the bed stand light and we propped Cory up against the headboard, spread his legs, and like two hungry nymphs, we lay between his legs, each taking a turn at sucking his limp dick to see if we could get it pumped again. Pretty soon he was up and ready to go. I wanted Kaylee to get what she was after, so I lay on my back at the other end of the bed, spread my legs, and began masturbating as I watched her mount his huge pole. She slowly squatted down on top of it as both watched me. Before long Kaylee was bouncing up and down, riding that thing like she was posting a trot on a horse. Seeing her breasts rise and fall, seeing the look on her face, seeing Cory's muscular hands holding her hips so that she didn't fly right off his joystick was too much for me. I squirted all over their bed as Kaylee came and came hard on Cory's dick.

Poor Cory didn't cum again. We all just sort of fell into place – Cory in the middle – and we drifted off to sleep. I reached down, unconsciously, between his legs during the night and felt how incredibly hard he was. I was soaking and – it's still a bit hazy to me – but I think I jilled it about two or three times with my right hand as my left hand held his cock in the darkness.

As she told me this, her hands were now rubbing the lotion into her thighs, between her legs, and around her pussy. "Oh, I'm so sore," she said. "When I woke up this morning, Kaylee was already out of the room and Cory was putting that big thing away in his boxers." There was a pause. "You're not mad. Are you,

Daddy?" She touched my hair and rubbed my arm.

"No, Lo. I'm not mad. So, things are fine with you and Kaylee?"

"Oh yeah. She knows I don't have any designs on Cory. It was all in good fun."

She sat for a while looking out the window. "There was something I wanted to ask you ...," she said eventually, "but I can't remem – oh yeah! That's it! What the hell was Erin doing in your bed last night?"

"Believe me, nothing as interesting as your story."

"No, what was she doing in your bed?"

You see, it's totally fine for Lo to spend the night philandering in her friends' bed, but she will cry bloody murder if any woman spent the night with me. I teased her for a bit – telling her to guess what we did and refusing to "kiss and tell," but eventually I recounted for her the odious conversation I had with Erin the previous night.

"Why," I asked Lo, "do you think she wanted to know all that?"

"It's obvious."

"Enlighten me."

"She is totally inhibited and needs to find some way of letting her freak-flag fly."

The Love Elite

All tallied, Lo came about four or five times in the car. I lost track. When we finally got home and had a few hours to ourselves before Erin and Steve's party, she brought me in the bedroom, first thing. She lay on the bed, spread eagle, and told me to get naked – an activity she loves to see. I obeyed diligently, for I was put into a state of distracted desperation by all her antics on the drive home. She said to me, "Admit you want to fuck me cause you're hard." Nothing gets Lo off like knowing that her body makes cock hard.

"No," I replied, "I want to fuck you cause you're easy."

I gave her what she wanted and as I did her, missionary style, she whispered in my ear, "Daddy, you know I'm yours – only yours. Yours is the only cock I want. Yours is the best. I love you. Cum in me. Mark me. Show me that I belong to you. Fill me up. Make me your cum-bucket. Make it so that I'm dripping your cum at the party tonight, reminding me that I'm yours and only yours. Give it to me, Daddy. I need it. I need it."

"No, Lo," I whispered back in her ear, "I'm not going to cum."

"Daddy, don't deny me."

She hates it when I refuse her my hot stream injection.

"Flip me over, Daddy, and fuck me like a dog."

"No, Lo, I want to make you cum like this first."

She spread her legs further apart, put her hand down between her legs on her clit and she stoked it hard, quickly flicking up and down. I could feel her straining fingers on the top of my shaft as I went in and out.

"Deep, Daddy, deep! Stay deep!"

I plunged in with all my weight and she convulsed and writhed and screamed. I felt something like a waterfall splashing between my legs.

"Now flip me over," she said after a moment, "and fuck me like I'm your bitch."

I did as she requested and as I did so she reached behind her and began fingering her ass. "Do you want to share me, Daddy? Do you want me to have one more in my ass?"

"Yes," was all I could manage to say.

She inserted her finger deep and said, "Do you want to feel another cock inside my ass like this – rubbing up against yours?"

"Yes," I panted.

"Do you want me to be filled up with cum and dripping from both holes?"

I slowed my thrusts. I tried to hold it in.

Lo knew what I was doing and what it meant. "That's it, Daddy," she said, "Let go. Let it go.

Go on. Fill me up. You know you want to. Go on." She's such a little succubus, hungry for warm cum.

She slid in her finger as far as it would go and was fingering herself frantically.

That was it. Loss of control. Practically loss of consciousness. I exploded in her as she was screaming, "I'm cumming! I'm cumming in my cunt! I'm cumming in my ass! Oh God! Yes!"

After a few moments of recovery, I said to her, "I hope you're happy."

"Oh, I am, Daddy," she replied with a smile.

"Well, that's it for me for the night."

We showered together and Lo said, "I want to suck your dick, Daddy."

(Indulge me for a moment while I reflect upon how much the addition of "Daddy" to the statement, "I want to suck your dick" makes that statement so much more ... *je ne sais quoi*.)

She got down on her knees in the shower and took my flaccid cock in her mouth, but to no avail.

Later, when we were in the car on our way to Erin's, I said to Lo, "So, what is this party all about?"

Lo said, "Erin just started her grad program and, since she's from the area and a lot of her classmates aren't, she's having a party to help them all feel more at home here. I think she also is inviting a bunch of our mutual friends from college who are still in the area. It should be fun."

I frowned.

"Awww, what's wrong, Daddy?"

"Nothing."

Lo reached over to tousle my hair with her fingers. "Come on, Daddy-O, tell me what's wrong."

"Is Cory going to be there?"

"Oh, is that it?" she asked with a laugh. "Yes, I think Cory and Kaylee said they'd be there too."

"Are you still jonesing for his cock?"

"Oh, Daddy."

"No, really, are you?"

"I told you, Daddy, it wasn't Cory, it was Kaylee I was 'jonesing' for."

"Well, that may be, but Cory certainly was a welcome fringe benefit."

You see, this cuckolding thing is complicated. On the one hand, Lo's lusting for cock – her unabashed longing for it, her exuberant search for ever bigger pieces of meat, her desire to be desired – turns me on. But, on the other hand, there is always the fear, the danger, the dread that she will find a cock, a man, a fuck that lures her away from me. It's not jealousy; it's insecurity. For years I've heard women say that exact same phrase, "I'm not jealous; I'm insecure," but it wasn't until I met Lo (and, in some ways our gender roles have been inverted) that I really, fully, experientially understood that feeling. At the same time, this flirting with this danger line makes the whole thing all-the-more exciting. It becomes an adrenaline rush – a high that is simultaneously incredibly uncomfortable and addictive. I suppose it is somewhat akin to what thrill riders seek with ever scarier rollercoasters, bungee jumping, skydiving, mountain climbing, etc. None of those activities are addictive the way cocaine or heroin is addictive, where there is a rush of absolute pleasure, but they are addictive in the way that running close to a precipice can create a natural high from vertigo. That's the best way to explain this kink for me.

Lo said to me, "My heart loves you, Daddy."

"But your puss wants everyone."

"Yeah, so?"

Well, that settled that.

As a result of our post-vacation copulation, shower, and Lo's trying on and rejecting three outfits before finally settling on the sexy little number (short skirt, jackpot top, black leather boots) she went with, we arrived at the party while it was in full swing. Steve and Erin live in a rented house in the burbs, complete with a basement, second floor, and a backyard.

A grill was fired up. A few coolers were out, stuffed full of beer, wine, and ice. A stereo was set up and playing music. People were milling about inside and out. How they managed to prepare for this party after driving back from the beach house was beyond me, but there it was and my spirits lifted when I saw the bottle of Crown Royal on the bar, half full.

Lo and I wriggled our way between guests. She got a glass of wine; I got a tumbler-full of whiskey on the rocks. From afar we spied Sally, and that dolt Jeff. Lo grabbed my hand and pulled me toward the backyard to forestall the inevitable interaction with them. In the back yard we met up with a bunch of Lo's old classmates from college whom she hadn't seen for some time (and wasn't too keen on seeing). We chatted and ate and chatted some more, mingling with new and old friends. Word clearly got out about this party because rather than the twenty or so people I was told would be there, there were at least forty to fifty young folk there. I was the grizzled grandfather, but the more whiskey I imbibed, the more the years felt like they were shedding off my true age.

The conversations and interactions we had during the party were not in any way memorable, except one. A friend of Erin's whom Lo knew in college, but never really liked, came up to Lo and pulled her aside saying, "So, you're dating Dr. H.?"

Lo said yes to the obvious.

"You know," this girl went on, "he was my professor too."

"Oh, really?"

"Yeah. I had *such* a crush on him. I mean, I've always wanted to have an affair with a professor, and if there was ever a professor I wanted to have an affair with, it would be Dr. H."

Lo had no idea how to respond to that. First, Lo had been dating me, officially, not on the side, for over three years. It wasn't an "affair." Second, this girl was being very presumptuous about when our relationship began. Third, Lo was suddenly feeling *very* possessive of her old man. He's *my* daddy, bitch. (She didn't say that, but I could hear her thinking it when she told me about the conversation later.) Lo just smiled politely and excused herself from the woman's presence.

As the night spun on, Lo and I drank a bit more excessively than planned. Alcohol is such a wily intoxicant; as soon as you hit the preset limit, then you feel like saying to hell with the limits. And that's exactly what I did. Let the limits be damned. Lo was more together than I and so she spoke to Erin and got the ok for us to spend the night. We continued our merriment and slowly the guests all seemed much more interesting, fun, and friendly. Just as slowly, the ranks of the guests began to thin. It was past midnight and what had been scores of people was now only about ten or twelve.

In addition to us and our hosts, Erin and Steve, there were several people we had just met that night, as well as Sally and Jeff, Cory and Kaylee, and an old friend of ours, Keith. Dan and Val didn't make it. We were all very inebriated and at one point, while watching some people play Beer-Pong, two of the female graduate students started making out. They were clearly doing it to attract the attention of a couple of guys there and Lo turned up her nose at them because, if there's one thing she can't stand, it's the playing of the "bi" card to impress men. Either that, or she was upset with me for gawking at their little tongue entwining tête-à-tête.

I followed Lo outside and there we encountered two graduate student guys who had suddenly come to fisticuffs. Nothing upsets Lo more than violence and her gut reaction to such displays of barbarity is to ... be very violent. She marched up to the two pugilists and immediately, unhesitatingly, tried to separate them. It was in vain and, luckily for all involved, the police had just pulled up and they broke up the fight, the party, and sent all people who could drive on their way.

When the dust settled, it turned out that a few couples had already taken up the bedrooms upstairs, a couple of other random folks had bunked for the night in the living room – on the couch or on the floor – and Erin told us that we could have one of the two full-sized beds in the basement. She and Steve would take the other.

It seemed that Erin was drunk, maybe high too, and she made some untoward remarks while showing us to our bed. She hopped into bed with Steve and shut off the lights saying, "So you won't be able to see what we're up to, you two pervs." I was already under the covers and Lo was silhouetted in the dim light from the door at the top of the stairs. She removed her shirt, her bra, and then her skirt and panties and hopped into bed naked next to me. Erin, from her comments, was eager for something to happen and before long, as I lay in the bed pulling at Lo's nipples, we heard the unmistakable sound of Erin and Steve fornicating in the bed next to us. Lo whispered in my ear to smack her pussy lips. "No Lo, not now."

"Yes, Daddy. Now."

I gave them one light slap.

Lo let out a long moan.

My palm was wet from her pussy.

"Again," she demanded.

I did it once more.

In what little light was available, we could see Erin on top of Steve moving back and forth on him. Lo turned and whispered in my ear, "Will you fuck me, Daddy?"

"I told you not to suck it out of me at home."

"Oh, come on!"

"No go."

"Phhhheeee," she said, perhaps an abbreviation of her Scarlett O'Hara "Fiddle-dee-dee."

They were going at it next to us and Lo was keen on getting some for herself. She turned on her back and began her usual autoerotic stimulation. But before she could get very far, suddenly, running down the stairs was our friend Keith. He jumped into our bed, fully clothed, and said, "Shhhh! Just let me stay here for a few." We had no idea what was going on. Then, only seconds later, another party goer came running down the stairs, turning on the lights as he did so. "Did any of you see Keith?"

Lo and I shook our heads no, as Keith hid below the covers.

"Shut out the lights," yelled Erin as she pulled the blankets over her naked body, riding cowboy on Steve.

"Sorry!" said the partygoer, as he shut off the switch and walked upstairs.

"Phew! Thanks!" said Keith from beneath the blankets, moving to get his head up above the covers.

Lo pushed his head back down and said, "Get under there." I could feel on my legs that she had spread hers and that Keith must have had his face in her crotch. I knew he was doing something down there because Lo was writhing with pleasure. Before long she was cumming (and Lo doesn't cum quietly). Then Lo went under the covers and did something, and I realized only later that she had taken off Keith's pants and, in a way that only she could do, had gotten a condom out of her bag and managed to put it on his erect cock. That girl is a magician, I tell you.

"Get in there," she said as she came back up above the covers.

Keith went at it between her legs and in only a couple of minutes Lo was cumming again. A couple of seconds after that and Keith was cumming. That's when I passed out.

When we woke up in the morning, Keith was gone, and Lo was holding me. I saw next to the bed a used condom – the only evidence that what I recalled from the previous night was not just a late-summer night's dream.

I saw Erin and Steve asleep in the bed next to us. I'm always an early riser and so I got up and snuck out of the bed, up the stairs, and fumbled around the kitchen to find the crucial items: coffee, coffee maker, mugs, and water. I brewed a pot and started cleaning up the awful mess. About a half-hour later Erin appeared.

"H.H., you don't have to do that."

"It's no trouble. I hope you don't mind, I helped myself to the coffee."

"No, of course not!"

"Is Lo still asleep?"

"I think so."

"And Steve too?"

"Oh yeah. He's not a morning person."

"So, did you have a good time last night? It was quite a party."

"I think so," she said.

"What do you mean?"

"Well, it kinda got out of hand. Police showed up, a fight, and ..."

She clearly wasn't fully awake yet. Some thought crossed her mind, and she wasn't sure about it.

"So many people slept over," she said, bemused by the sleeping guests in the living room and upstairs.

I was putting what trash I had collected in the garbage and pulled it out, asking her where she'd like me to put it.

"Oh, in the garage is fine."

I carried it out and when I returned, she rushed up to me with a look of concern on her face. "What happened last night?" she asked, pulling in close to me.

"There was a fight, the police came ..."

She interrupted me, "No, not that. I mean, downstairs."

"Lo and I went to bed in one bed and you and Steve went to bed in the other."

"Did you ...? Never mind."

"Did we hear you fucking?" I finished her question for her, unconcerned about whether it made her uncomfortable or not.

She turned away. "Oh God! You did."

"You weren't very discrete about it."

"Stop!"

She turned toward me. "Did Keith get in your bed at some point?"

I nodded.

"What happened?"

"I'm not sure. He came downstairs, hopped in our bed, I fell asleep, and in the morning he wasn't there."

"Did Lo ...?"

"What do you think?"

She put her hand to her mouth, as if in shock.

"In the bed with you?" she asked in a hushed voice.

I nodded.

"I can't believe that!" She was looking at me intently. "Wha...?" She began to formulate a question, but it dangled in the air without being asked.

"You want to know details?"

She looked at me at first as if I were about to tell her all, but then she realized the full force of the question.

"No, no."

"It's ok, Erin," I said, switching into kindly mentor mode, "you're suffering from a classic case of Leontius' conflict."

"From what?"

"In Plato's *Republic,* he speaks of a man named Leontius who, upon returning to Athens, sees along his way a pile of executed criminals' lifeless, naked bodies outside the city walls. His conscious mind is appalled by the sight, but his more prurient, subconscious impulses impel him toward the horrific sight until he stands before the pale white corpses and screams at his eyes,

'Look, you wicked devils, feast yourselves on the beautiful sight!'"

"That's a horrible story!"

"Yes, but it gets at truth of what you're experiencing: attraction/repulsion or allure/revulsion. You are fascinated by Lo and our lifestyle, but you think you despise it. You judge her but want to know more."

"Ridiculous!"

"Really? You seemed to be quite the little sexhibitionist last night. I mean, not even Lo put on a show like you did."

She laughed nervously. She picked up some beer bottles and emptied them out in the sink. She turned to me and said, "So, did Lo like sleeping with him?"

I said, "Like I said, I fell asleep right after and I don't know where he disappeared to, but this morning Lo whispered in my ear that he was really, really small. Very disappointing for her, though he did the trick."

She looked at me and said, "That doesn't surprise me. I mean he's a tiny little man. He looks like a boy, a leprechaun."

"Lo lusts for a big cock – like Cory's – but has yet to find the elusive Moby Dick."

She looked over at me and I answered the question she was thinking but didn't ask. "I'm well endowed, but, I'll admit, not the biggest Lo's ever had. And I certainly am not that massive meat she dreams of."

"Oh my God!" she exclaimed, "She's such a slut!"

"Be careful how you use that term," I said, getting way too philosophical for such an early Sunday morning. "It's a fine term if you're using it subversively, but if you mean it in the way that patriarchy has intended it then ..."

"What the hell are you talking about?"

"Yeah, I guess it is too early for this. I'm beginning to sound like Lo. You're right. She's a slut, but she's my slut and I love her."

Not long after I said this, Lo staggered up the stairs.

Lo and I said our good-byes and hopped in the car before most of the other partygoers had woken from their slumbers.

On the way home, Lo asked about my conversation with Erin. I told her about it and again she too put the question to me, "Daddy, do you think I'm a slut?"

"Yes, Lo, I do."

"Good."

When we got home, we took a long hot bath together and then we got into bed, hung-over, tired, and ready to collapse.

Lo held me close, and she asked me, "Daddy, do you think I'm a nympho?"

I was contemplating the question and before I formulated an answer, Lo had already fallen asleep.

I slept too, for a little while, but I got up and something about the strange weekend on the beach, the party, all of Erin's persnickety questions, and Lo's quiet wondering as she drifted off got me thinking again about that touchstone (if outdated, prejudiced, paternalistic, patronizing, and profoundly benighted) book, *Nymphomania: a Study of the Oversexed Woman*, by Albert Ellis and Edward Sagarin. I grabbed the book off my shelf and read the last few pages again:

A few women seem to reject social condemnation and hold high self-esteem while asserting their rights to a free sex life. For these women, one writer (Hirsch, Arthur H., *The Love Elite*, New York, Julian Press, 1963) utilizes the phrase, 'the love elite.' A woman who belongs to this group, Hirsch contends, understands that she is free; and the love elite woman is capable of accepting responsibility with freedom. She makes her own distinction between the rational and irrational demands of society:

In love and in sexual relationships she demands to be free. She has asserted her equality with the man – has rejected once and for all an inferior 'second sex' status. She accepts no authority determining her use of her body or mind. Her affections and her intimacies henceforth will be freely bestowed – or not bestowed at all.

Thus, she is sometimes at odds with society's values – values still based upon a time when woman was subordinate. Because she has gone beyond society's values – truly risen above them – her 'indiscretions' may lead her into difficulties. But if difficulties arise, they are less catastrophic because she knows, or believes that the values of society – not her own – are at fault.

America and the Western world must still make long strides toward the emancipation of women. Such emancipation will not exist until a female has the right to choose to have lovers as a man so chooses, and until she lives in a group that does not inflict upon her the notion that she is a fallen woman when she loves freely.

A few women suffer from nymphomania or compulsive promiscuity. But many more suffer from lack of sexual freedom, from condemnation of their free lives, and from pressures to survive and retain a healthy self-image in an inegalitarian atmosphere. When sexually alive women are fully accepted, and are not considered over-sexed trollops, much of the anguish will be relieved. This will be a great stride toward implementing the progress made in the last century regarding economic and political liberation of woman.

As I reread this uncharacteristically insightful passage, I thought about Lo and Erin. I also wondered why this Arthur Hirsch and his book, *The Love Elite*, is nowhere to be found. I've done extensive research and have yet to get my hands on it. Is it a conspiracy? While pondering these things, Lo sauntered into the living room, naked, and curled up next to me and snuggled under the throw. She saw the book in my hands. I read the passage to her and said in response to her question, "Lo, to some you might be a nympho, but to me you really are an example *par excellence* of the love elite."

Every Morning...

The other day I was driving in my car and on the radio was playing Sugar Ray's, "Every Morning." As I listened to this old familiar song that I had heard countless times before, it dawned on me for the first time, "Every morning there's a halo hanging from the corner of my girlfriend's four-post bed." The halo – it's hers. It's hanging there cause she takes it off at night. She's a little devil in the sack. She puts it on again in the morning and goes out to work, like an angel. My obtuse little mind had cracked the simple imagery of this pop tune and ... AND, I realized it's about my Lo. That describes her to a tee. She wakes up, masturbates, showers, masturbates, gets dressed, puts on her halo, saunters off to work, frequently masturbates at work when no one is watching, comes home, cums at home, cums and cums again. Sleep, repeat. And no one is any the wiser. At night she might go down on a stranger in the car. Other nights she may bed a lovely woman. And just about every day she poses for lascivious photos that she posts on the internet. Yet, by day, no one – except those other freaks with an eye for freak-flags – sees her freaky-deeky-crazy-nympho-slut-whore ways.

Take, for instance, the fact that she is, by profession, an advocate for safe, healthy, consensual sex. Yet, at night, when she comes home from work, she'll get down on all fours, ask me to put a leash around her neck, lead her by it through the house to the bedroom, have her sit on her knees and beg for my bone, before taking it in her mouth and being pet on the head and told she's a "good girl." She then hops up on the bed and pleads to be taken. I tell her, "You know, it's wrong for us to do this," indulging her fetish for role-playing as I slowly slide my rod in her and she whispers, "I love you, Daddy." I service her that way for a while, until she cums a couple of times, and then I pull out, and slowly, gently, carefully insert my sex drive made flesh in her other orifice, per her request, until she demands that I ram it home. All the while she cries out her pet name for me – "Daddy, Daddy, Daddy" – with each painful thrust. She tells me to make her a dirty girl and says she wants my shaft back in her hungry and vacuous cunt. I oblige and, as if in lust for two cocks at once, she has me shift back-and-forth and back-and-forth, front-to-back and back-to-front again, before begging me to cum in her mouth and licking me clean, as I heap upon her the worst, most depraved names I can possibly invent.

And then, when we're done with our little charade, I lie on my back, put my arm around her shoulders, pull her close and tight to me, kiss her forehead ever-so-gently and say, "Goodnight, Lo. I love you."

Already drifting off to dreamland, she murmurs back, almost inaudibly, "I love you too."

My little nymph-devil.

Nude, Not Naked

Pulling into the apron of the five-star hotel, we quickly realized that this was not the resort by the beach we had imagined. Its proportions were immense. Yes, we had seen images of its golf course, its proximity to the ocean, its rooms, but we had no idea that the hotel would be a conglomerate of four separate buildings, each three stories tall, shaped in a rectangular fashion enclosing the pool, hot tub, and fire pit. The buildings were so large that you needed to either drive or call one of the hotel staff to pick you up in a golf cart to get from your hotel room to the dining room. Our first instinct was to cancel the reservations and find a B&B somewhere down the road, but the likelihood of a vacancy was slim to none during this peak season.

So, we checked in, happy to be on our own, finally, with no sneaking around the stray cousin who had been our suite companion for the first leg of our vacation. We had a late dinner and then, exhausted from the drive, I collapsed on the bed in a light coma as Lo, frustrated, rubbed one out next to me. I had no knowledge of it until she told me about the following morning in her seductive "Fuck me now, Daddy," tone of voice. But the next morning I was not quite ready for her, and I kept her pleadings at bay.

After a small breakfast, we went out by the pool for a quick dip and to have a couple of mimosas in the sun. As we were lying out by the pool Lo said to me, "Look."

"What?" I said, waking up from the beginnings of a nap.

"Look, there."

She nodded, and by that gesture she pointed out two youths in the pool nestled by the edge, arms entwined, oblivious to everyone around them.

"What?" I asked.

"They're totally doing it," she said in disgust.

"What?"

"Yes, they are."

I observed them closely for a few minutes. He had his back up against the wall and she was wrapped around him, her head buried in the curve of his neck and shoulders. They undulated slowly as children and adults played and swam around them.

"Get a room!" Lo said, audibly, but not audibly enough for the lovers to hear.

"Oh Lo, let them have their fun."

"No. That's disgusting."

As we bickered about it and watched, others noticed too.

The guy looked around briefly and pushed his girlfriend away for a moment. But like two magnets of opposite polarities, they were soon intertwined again. This time she was against the wall and he in front. I got up to get a towel from the bin and I purposely walked close to them and took a good look. As I did, it became obvious to me what was happening: he was fingering her and, just as I walked by, she looked up at me and her face became all contorted and she screamed just loud enough for me to hear. As I passed them, I heard him say with relief, "Finally!" as if he had been trying to make her cum for some time now.

I returned to Lo on the chaise lounge and passed a towel to her and took one for myself. I wrapped mine around my shoulders. She put hers over her lap. I reported to her what I saw and heard. She haughtily turned up her nose at the couple and shook her head in judgment of them.

"Oh Lo, come off it," I said, "You know you're only upset cause you wish it was you."

She turned away from me with the same look of opprobrium as she displayed about the couple in the pool.

As she was lying on her back in her dark shades, I said, "Lo."

"What?" she asked without sitting up.

"Now look!"

She sat up and saw the couple on the other side of the pool, the guy with his back to the wall again and his girlfriend in front of him. They were kissing.

"Yeah, so?"

"She's repaying the favor."

"What?!"

People-watching can be so much fun.

"Yeah, she's jerking him off."

Lo looked more closely. Sure enough, I was right.

Lo didn't criticize this time. I wondered about her lack of commentary and when I looked over at her, I saw she had set her recliner at a 45-degree angle and that she was watching the couple as her right hand made a small bulge popping up and down under her towel over her lap.

"Lo, your naughty!" I said, assuming the same high-and-mighty tone she had used only moments earlier.

She ignored me.

Before either she or he could complete the attendant deed, the couple got called by someone who appeared to be the mother of one of them. Oh, how dreadful! The mother was in a great rush, but there was no way for him to gracefully exit the pool. They made excuses, but ultimately, he had to get out and he walked right past Lo and me to quickly grab a towel from the bin. Lo looked with lust at his ginormous protuberance as he passed. The wicked girl (Lo, that is) continued with her morning masturbation session even after the wicked couple had left the scene. Once I saw her face grimace – the way the girl's did earlier – I said, "OK, Lo, fun time is over. We have a vacation to attend to."

She looked at me sheepishly and looked around to ascertain whether she had an audience, and then she got up carefully. When we got back to the hotel room, I saw that she had made a little wet mark in the crotch of her bikini bottoms.

She slipped them off and slipped on a sheer blue blouse. "I'm gonna go commando cause I'd just have to change my panties two or three times otherwise."

That day we hit the road early to make the three-hour trek down the coast road to the famous Hearst Castle. All the way there Lo did her best to distract me (and the other drivers) by putting her sexy, smooth legs up on the dash of the convertible as we drove with the top down, spreading those delectable gams, and tanning her inner (pantiles) thighs in the fresh, sea air. Occasionally she massaged her clean-shaven puss, and more than once she inserted one and then two fingers to bring herself to an orgasm.

"Do you want to get us killed?!" I rebuked her.

"Pish-posh," she said dismissively.

"Lo, cut it out," I insisted, "this road is dangerous enough without your trying to divert my eye to your devilish shenanigans!"

As I said this, a wicked smile crossed her face, and she looked out over the hood of the car at the oncoming car that almost went out of its lane and swerved into us. It would have been curtains for all of us if the poor sop driving didn't get ahold of himself and remember that it's a 400-foot sheer drop into the Pacific *and*, even worse, his wife is right next to him watching, judging, and plotting her revenge for the inevitable dalliance of his eye soaking in the spread legs cumming in the opposite direction!

"Put that thing away and stop being such a brat."

"But Daddy, you showed it no attention last night or this morning," she said with her characteristic pout, ignoring me and continuing to fondle herself.

That pretty much sums up the three hours of death-defying driving down Rt. 1 that morning.

I was very relieved when we finally arrived at our destination intact. We got our tickets and up we went to the legendary Xanadu.

There, amid the opulence and grandeur of the palace in the sky, Lo and I strolled the gardens, sauntered in the great rooms, and stood in silence looking over the feint clouds down to the distant sea below. The aromas of all the fruit-bearing trees and the sound of hummingbirds made it a romantic indulgence of the senses. Everywhere one looked, one's eyes were greeted by a stunning vista, a delightful arrangement of flowering florae, and whimsically care-free statues of naked women and men, nymphs, satyrs, and gods in all their alabaster glory. I poked my camera at several of the sculptures in the garden and snapped some shots. Lo looked at me, jealous that these inanimate objects had temporarily distracted my attention from her, and said, "Daddy, you only like these because they're naked."

"Lo, they're nudes. Not naked. There is a difference."

This hedonic surrounding of the senses with every conceivable pleasure revved Lo's engine to the point that she was practically cumming standing up in her flowing blue skirt. "Oh, Daddy," she said at one point when we were partially concealed behind an orange tree in a small grotto, as she put her hand between my legs, "Let me get on my knees and have you in my mouth. Just for a moment."

"Lo, there are ..."

"Just for one quick lick!" She was already on her knees, trying to unzip my pants.

"Lo!"

She just looked up at me and licked her chops.

"Lo, you stand up! You hear me?!" I said in the firmest whisper I could muster.

She knew that this tone meant no fooling around and she got up, but she was on the lookout for a place to steal away.

Gradually, as the noon-time breeze gave way to a hot sun, we found shade under the lovely arbor by the Neptune pool. Conveniently the curators of this palatial public space placed lounge chairs for people to sit and imagine that they were William's guests in the days of Chaplin and Garbo. As we sat, Lo was up to her pranks again. Slowly she let the hem of her skirt slip up her thigh as she put her legs up on the lounge chair, exposing herself to the visitors across the pool from us and to those who were walking by directly in front of her.

When I caught this naughtiness, I scolded her and she said, "Oh Daddy, you're simply no fun on this trip," but at least she put her legs flat.

Suffice it to say that the trip back up the coast was as dangerous and distracting as the way down. Along the way we stopped at a wonderful restaurant overlooking the cliffs and ocean set up like a bird's perch atop the jagged Big Sur steeples. We got there just in time to witness the sunset and sit outside as the clouds rolled in below us off the ocean mists. Lo looked fabulous and her serene beauty was stiff competition to Nature's own. Though I had been refusing and rebuking her all day, my defenses were growing weak and my desires increasing.

After our meal, I sped it the rest of the way through the windy terrain till we got to the more conventional straightaway by Carmel. Once we were out of danger and covered by the darkness (though neither mattered much to Lo), Lo went down on me, far down, – with the top still down! Up she popped for air now and again as we drove through the little hamlet.

Once we got back to the hotel, Lo and I hopped in the spacious tile and glass encased shower together. She was gorgeous with the water streaming down her breasts and over her already wet pussy. I kissed and caressed her, sucked her nipples, and got down on my knees. "Daddy," she said.

"What Lo?"

"Daddy, I have to pee."

"Go right ahead," I said with a grin.

She did so as I cupped my hand between her legs and let her warm waters dribble all down my arm and chest.

I then stood up and turned her around and fucked her from behind till she came twice, screaming at the top of her lungs. This is what she had been waiting for all day and all the previous night.

We got out, dried off, and then she put on her bikini. I knew instantly what she wanted. We walked over to the pool area, but first we had to pass the fire pit. There were a few couples sitting around it, talking. We nodded hello to them. In the pool was a dad and his two daughters. They looked like college sorority girls on vacation with their divorced father before the new school year began. Lo unwrapped her towel, revealing her bikini-clad bod, and we both took a quick dip in the pool. I noticed that the dad's eyes were following Lo and Lo was doing everything in her power to keep them on her.

Lo swam over to me and wrapped me in her arms the way the kids that morning had been. She reached down between my legs underwater and said, "Oh, Daddy." Yes, it's true, I couldn't conceal my arousal. She reached into my bathing suit and stroked my hard cock a bit. "How are you going to get out?" she asked.

"Get out?"

"Yeah," she said, "I want to get warm in the hot tub."

It wasn't easy, but I slithered out of the pool, and we went to the vacant hot tub. The two bodies of water were connected by a narrow path that had various plants lined along it, so there was some relative privacy there, yet it was totally exposed to the three floors of hotel rooms that surrounded us on every side. I eased into the steamy and bubbly tub and, as I sat in the soupy concoction, I looked up at Lo through the steam and, to my great surprise, I saw her slip out of her bikini and quickly step into the little kidney-shaped pool.

She sidled right up to me and took my hand and placed it between her legs as she placed her hand between mine. There we were: she naked as the day she was born under the bubbles, and I with my very eager member desiring to take her, but inhibited, first by my bathing suit, second by my mind. But we were not destined to have at it just yet. The dad from the pool (predictably) followed us to the hot tub and he slowly descended into it, smiling at Lo.

There was no way he could see her naked body through the swirl of bubbles, but before long, he was up to his shoulders in water and he casually looked around him, trying to pretend that he wasn't looking at Lo, and I marked that his eyes took note of Lo's bikini lying in plain sight next to the tub. A grin slowly evolved on his lips, but just as quickly it disappeared as his two girls joined us in the tub. Uncomfortable moment for dear old dad. No?

After about fifteen minutes of this, the father said to his girls, "It's almost ten and the pool closes soon. You'd better get your towels and get to bed."

"What about you?" one of them asked.

"I'll be right along," he said – sly dog.

The girls got out and dried off their long, nubile bodies and scurried out of the pool area. From a distance, we heard the chain fence close. Now it was just the three of us and Lo, cock hungry as she is, was not interested in this man or his cock. Yes, that's right, I repeat, she was not interested. She only had eyes (and puss) for me that night. She was feeling romantic, not horny; loving, not lustful. She wanted *her* daddy, not just any daddy, though I suspect the attention of this other man wasn't totally met with displeasure. She's an attention whore as well as a cock whore.

She started kissing me, open mouth and nibbling my earlobe, running her tongue down my neck. She was very, very close to me and I suppose that eventually the other dad got the message, because he got out of the tub and walked away without our having to say a word. (It will be noted that Lo did look up to see if he was erect and, yes, dear reader, the answer is, he was. Very.)

After he left, we had the place to ourselves. It was lovely – surrounded by exotic flora, the lights from the bottom of the hot tub illuminating the blue and white bubbly waters, the stars overhead, and hundreds of windows from the four quadrants of the hotel looking in on us. Lo pulled my cock out of my shorts, and she descended under the water to take it in her mouth. I felt her hands guiding it onto her tongue and then I felt the soft lips close upon it as she took it back and forth, in and out of her mouth. The contrast between the slight roughness of her tongue and the thousands of frantic bubbles in the water was sublime.

She popped up to catch her breath and ask, "You like, Daddy?"

"Oh yeah," I said as an eager look crossed her face just before she descended for a second round. She was down below the churning chaos, and I had dropped my head back to enjoy the erotic mouth massage with my eyes closed when suddenly an unusual flicker of lights played upon the screen of my eyelids. I opened my eyes and was momentarily blinded by a bright light pouring on me in the night. Had I died? Was the heat of the water and the delectable sensation of Lo's lips too much for my old ticker to take? Was I going to the proverbial light? No, it turned out. Rather, there was a night patrolman with his flashlight beaming on me like a spotlight in the theater. He stood only a few feet away. Before either of us could say anything, Lo suddenly popped up from between my legs and blurted out, "How'm I doing, Daddy? I can really hold my breath, huh?"

When she wiped the water from her eyes, she realized something was not right and she turned around, only to be temporarily blinded, as I was. The officer, it's true, had caught us. But Lo's use of her special name for me had caught the officer in quite the uncomfortable moment. After a pause of an interminably long silent, dumbfounded, stare, he said, "Folks, I'm going to have to ask you to leave. It's 10:30 and the pool area closed half an hour ago."

Lo looked at me. We were a bit stuck. In her enthusiastic Jaques Cousteau explorations underwater, Lo had removed my suit completely. I had no idea what she had done with it. It could have been chewed to a shredded mess by the strong pump at the bottom of the pool for all I knew. But luckily, Lo rescued me by passing the shorts into my hands underwater. This didn't solve her dilemma, however.

I slid on my bathing suit underwater (backwards, it so turned out) and got up and out. I grabbed a towel nearby and opened it up for Lo. She, like a water-nymph, slowly emerged from the blue and white churning soup, water glistening and cascading down her smooth skin – naked from head to toe. The officer, unaware of his actions, shined the flashlight at the focus of his attention and so there was a slow down and up movement of the light covering every inch of Lo's sexy body as he took in her visage and mentally recorded every inch of it for his own stimulation later when he would be alone in the security house.

I passed the towel to Lo and she wrapped it around herself. Slowly she bent over to pick up her discarded bikini (flashing the officer from beneath her towel hem, for one last treat) and we sauntered out of the pool area, giggling like children, waiving hello at the few folks left by the fire pit.

Up we went to our room and there we got naked again and went into the warm shower. As the water beat down upon us, I got down on my knees and began covering Lo with kisses below the waist. But, before long, she grabbed me and said, "No, stop."

"Why?" I asked, looking up at her.

"I have to pee again!"

"Go right ahead," I said.

She looked down at me and, she shook her head "no."

"You can do it," I said, encouragingly.

She shook her head again in the hot water.

"Go on."

She could withhold it no longer. Out shot a strong, hot, golden stream down upon my torso, accompanied by a long sigh of relief from Lo. When she was done, I slowly slid up her wet, smooth body and kissed her open-mouthed under the showerhead. Then I forcefully turned her around and entered her from behind and, as her arms supported her on the wall under the showerhead, I repeatedly thrust forward into her. Moments later she was screaming with delight. Her legs were so tired, weak, and unstable afterward, that she had to sit on the floor of the shower and recover.

I stood under the shower looking down at her.

"Jack it," she commanded.

I took my manhood in hand and did as she commanded.

She spread her legs and began stroking her swollen, red pussy lips.

I was no longer hard as I held myself.

"Come on, Daddy-O, can't you get it up?"

I smirked.

"What?"

"It's my turn," I said.

She knew what I meant. "Go ahead."

"You sure?"

"Very," she said as she spread her legs and put her head back. I then returned the favor she had bestowed upon me twice that night, completely drenching her like Gulliver extinguishing the Empress' palace fire in Lilliput. She squirmed and wiggled as her finger wagged between her legs.

I then recommenced with her bidding, taking my own matters in hand, and she watched me the way she watches porn. She asked me to back up and adjust the shower head so that it beat down right on her puss, causing her to come with convulsions.

When we dried off, she threw on an oversized sweatshirt because the night had turned chilly. I was wearing only my flannel pajama bottoms. We lay in bed for a while kissing and caressing each other until finally I took her out onto the balcony that overlooked the pool area of the courtyard in the center of the four quadrants of the hotel buildings. There, on the balcony, I lowered my pajama pants to around my thighs and I turned Lo, so she was bent over, leaning on the balcony railing with her arms, facing out into the courtyard and the hotel room windows across from us. I slowly entered her from behind, just as I had done in the shower. But now, instead of hot, steamy beads of water beating down upon us, there was a dry, cool breeze flowing over us. My hands caressed Lo under her sweatshirt and I slowly slid my hands up and down her sides and cupped her breasts. Then I began to pull the sweatshirt up, inch-by-inch, till it revealed her ass and puss. A little higher and it revealed her tum. I went to go a little higher and she turned and said, "No."

I ignored her. It was a soft no and not a hard, full-stop no. I slowly slid it up and finally off her till she was standing naked on the balcony facing hundreds of windows and being fucked from behind. Her nipples were erect and hard, titillated by chill of the air in contrast with the heat of the shower, and pulled and pinched by my probing fingertips. We went at it like that for a good long time until she had to swallow her screams lest her climactic aria reverberate throughout the acoustic chamber created by the rectangular hotel courtyard area. When she had fully cum, and her squirting had dribbled down both her and my inner thighs, she fell to her knees, and I gave my manhood a couple of strong tugs before ejaculating in her mouth and on her face.

"Did you like, Daddy," she said, when we were comfortably tucked into bed.

"Oh yeah," I said, as I slowly drifted off.

"What did you like, Daddy?"

"I liked getting you naked on the balcony, Lo."

After a moment, during which time I had already entered into a dream, she said, "I was nude, Daddy, not naked."

"Oh no, Lo," I replied from out of my dream, "You were naked. Very naked."

Lola's Lysistrata

No!" she said.

"Why?" I asked.

"You know very well why," she said, turning around, standing on her tiptoes, and pushing out her naked bum. "If you want this," she added, slapping her ass for emphasis, "then you're going to have to earn it."

A little backstory here is in order. We were in a fight. Lo was upset with me. She was more than upset with me. She was furious with me. I had recently hired a red-headed, buxom, bombshell of a woman to do Public Relations for my business. The fact that she was a red-headed buxom bombshell was most certainly *not* the reason I had hired her. She had an impressive résumé, impeccable credentials, and stellar recommendations. She had found *me* via LinkedIn and had offered her services to me at just the time when I was thinking of expanding my business into a new market. In short, there were very good and eminently rational reasons to hire this woman, none of which had to do with her looks. But Lo couldn't get beyond the surface appearance.

"A ruby red Jessica Rabbit?! Really? You just had to have a complete set, didn't you?"

"What are you talking about?" I asked, genuinely perplexed.

"Your secretary is a blonde bimbo."

"She's *not* a bimbo."

"Your PR person is a ginger. And I'm brunette. You've got all your bases covered."

"Lo, that has nothing to do with it. Sheer coincidence."

"Really?"

"Yes, really. I'm not even attracted to redheads."

"All three of your previous girlfriends were redheads."

"Exactly my point."

"You're not making sense."

"All my exes are redheads. I broke up with them. Clearly red is not my color."

"Well, no sex for you until you fire her."

"I can't just fire her. That would be a violation of her rights."

"What about my rights?" she said, thumbing her chest.

"What about them?"

"Don't I have the right to peace of mind, quiet enjoyment, not to mention, my conjugal rights?"

"Lo, I'm ready to conjugate right now," I said, pulling out my hard cock.

"Phhhht," she replied, "Not until Jessica Rabbit is gone."

Just to be clear, dear reader, the new PR person was not named Jessica, but for the purposes of this story, we'll stick with Lo's derogatory name for her.

"I know you're a jealous woman but ..." I began, trying to restate my defense.

"What sort of PR professional posts pics of herself in a thong bikini on the beach on her Instagram page?"

"You looked up her Instagram page?"

"Of course, I did. And I know you did too!"

"I most certainly did not. But can I see?"

That little attempt at humor was ill timed. Lo put on her panties and work clothes and walked out of the room in her heels as she lifted her right hand to flip me the bird as she slammed the door behind her and called out, "NO SEX FOR YOU!"

I know that Lola wasn't thinking rationally because what sense does it make for a nymphomaniac to go on a sex strike to get her way? Nonetheless, she was upset. Very upset. And somehow, I had to make things right. But I didn't know how. Would she eventually come around? Would I have to dismiss Jessica? Would they have a knock down drag out cat fight? Who knows.

One thing I was confident about was that Lo wouldn't last long with this protest of hers. How could she? Unless she was going to go out there and find someone else to bang, which was always a distinct possibility.

Two, then three, then four days (and nights!) went by, and she stuck to her guns. I wasn't even allowed to sleep in the same bed with her, but I was subjected to her moans and groans of self-pleasure. A tantalizing torture.

After the fifth day of this cruel and very unusual punishment, I could take no more. I had come up with a strategy for winning the war. I put things into place and two days later, Monday afternoon, my secret weapon arrived by mail in a non-descript cardboard box, about the size of a shoebox. It had my name on it and I purposefully left it out on the dining room table for Lo to ponder like Pandora's Box.

Like clockwork, when Lo got home and saw it, she asked, "What's that?"

"Oh, just something for me that I ordered on-line," I replied nonchalantly.

"What is it?" she asked again, picking up the box and shaking it.

"Don't shake it!" I warned.

"Is it fragile? Is it for me?"

"It's really none of your concern," I said, knowing how much that would piss her off.

"What the fuck is it?! You'd better tell me right now."

"Calm down," I said. "You'll find out soon enough."

"I'll find out this instant!" she said, stomping her little foot.

"It's just ... just something to help me out."

"Help you out? How? Is it a lifetime supply of Viagra?"

"Darling, I certainly don't need any E.D. medicines."

"That's what you think."

"But you are on the right track."

"That's it, I'm opening it up," she said, making for the kitchen to get scissors.

She returned and violated the sacred law of the postal service – opening another's mail. And when she saw what was inside, she flipped out! All going to plan.

"Stoya the Destroya Signature Fleshlight!"

"Yes," I said calmly, talking the box from her hands. "If you're going on a sex-strike, then I'll just have to take matters into my own hands," I said.

"A surrogate pussy?! You throw that thing out right now! I will not stand for it!"

"Then get on your back and spread your legs for me."

"No."

"OK then," I said, turning to leave with my pussy in hand.

"Where are you going?"

"To get laid."

"The hell you are!"

I walked into the bedroom, removed my clothes, took Stoya's pussy out of the box, read the extensive instructions and warnings, and began to follow the directions. I was pleased to see that it came with its own small bottle of lube.

Lo walked in. (I hadn't locked the door.)

"You're really going to fuck that thing?" she asked.

"Care to watch?" (I knew that she wouldn't or couldn't resist.)

She sat on the side of the bed as I stroked lube all over my hard cock. I then put lube on my fingers and began fingering Stoya.

"What are you doing?" she asked, perplexed.

"The instructions clearly say to lubricate the inside before use."

"Wouldn't you rather something that's naturally wet?" she asked as she removed her panties. She still had on her heels from work and her black dress. She spread her legs on the bed and pulled at her pussy lips.

"Of course, I would," I said, "but Stoya is primed and ready for me." (I was purposefully being an asshole.)

"I've been primed and ready. Wouldn't you rather pump this," she asked as she slipped in a couple of fingers.

"Are you really offering?"

"No. You can't have it. I'm mad at you."

"OK then," I said as I penetrated Stoya's soft and supple pussy. I had two hands on the casing of the Fleshlight and I was sliding it on and off my cock as Lo fingered her own puss with one hand and then really upped the ante by fingering her ass and saying, "Is Stoya tight?"

"Yeah," I said.

"As tight as my little ass?"

"I doubt it."

"Do you want my ass?" she asked, fingering both her holes in front of me as I looked on hungrily.

I continued fucking Stoya, imagining I was fucking Lola. "You know, there's a Stoya anal Fleshlight as well," I said.

"Then fuck that, because you can say goodbye to these!" she retorted as she turned around on the bed, so she was lying on her tum, her head propped up by her hands. I could still see her ass as her dress was flapped up over her waist. I knew that something Lo loves is seeing guys masturbate. She frequently requested that I jack it for her, and she can never get enough since she can't both watch me and have me. That's why she wants two men at the same time.

I did as she commanded and slid the pussy down and back on my rod. I could see her grow visibly jealous of the device.

"What?" I said at her displeasure, "You have your Hitachi, your double-ended-dildo, your Remus, your ..."

"Shut up and cum already," she said.

"And you're jealous of me because once, ONCE, in however many years I get a sex toy for myself?!"

"What about your sheath? Your penis extender?"

"That was for you, not me."

"Enough dialogue. Fuck that pussy and cum if you're gonna cum."

"If you really want me to cum," I said, "then hold it for me."

"You want me to hold Stoya's pussy so you can fuck her instead of me?"

"Well, are you willing to give me your pussy?"

She reached out and held onto the thick trunk of the sleeve. I fucked more vigorously. Her mouth opened. At the crucial moment, I pulled out and, without warning, ejaculated the money shot all over her delighted face. She was dripping in my cum when she said, "That. Was. Amazing."

Deep-C Fishing

I had just returned from a week-long fishing trip with three of my friends. For the record, I despise fishing. Fishing is for people who want to be in nature but who don't know how simply to *be* in nature – without purpose, goal, or utilitarian project. I am not of their ilk. The silver lining to this trip was that it was up in the mountains, on a lake, in a log cabin. The downside to this trip was that there was absolutely no wi-fi within a twenty-mile radius of where we were staying. That meant no communication with Lo for a week!

I was nearly beside myself needing a fix of her lovely skin, her soft touch, her caress. I didn't even have her voice to sustain me. No gradual withdrawal from her, my drug of choice. No substitute for her intoxicant. The closest I could get was a specially curated set of photos I had of her stored on my phone. "Favorites."

We did get radio and this classic rock song played, mocking my predicament:

I'm outta luck, outta love
Got a photograph, picture of
Passion killer, you're too much
You're the only one I want to touch
I see your face every time I dream
On every page, every magazine

So wild and free so far from me
You're all I want, my fantasy
Yes, I missed her. I craved her. I wanted to praise her. And I did, telling my friends what I could about my little nymph, without revealing too much or our special dalliances that are reserved just for us – oh, and all of you, our lovely reading public.

At night, I set up her image on my phone and sat at my computer to write sexy, sensual stories to her, for her, about her. I dreamt of the naughty things she was doing while I was away. I would look at the photos as lyrics from a song filtered in from the other room:
Photograph I don't want your
Photograph I don't need your
Photograph all I've got is a photograph
But it's not enough
My pals knew how devoted to Lo I was, but they were unaware of how free I allow her to be. One of them walked in while I was writing. Seeing my phone on the desk next to me with Lo's image on it, he casually picked it up. I made as if to protest, but I didn't protest too much. He looked at the photos I had of her – naughty photos – and shared his discovery with the others. They ridiculed me, ribbed me, and teased me for my Playboy internet pornstar.

Even the radio mocked me with the lyrics:
You can't imagine what your image means.
The pages come alive.
Your magic greets everyone who reads.

Heart-break in overdrive
Are you for real, it's so hard to tell,
from just a magazine.
Yeah, you just smile and the picture sells,
look what that does to me.

One night, after many shots of whiskey, they eventually pried out of me a confession of her sins. They sat, wide-eyed, hard-up, and enraptured by the stories I spun. At first, they doubted, then they shouted, and finally they pouted. They wanted *her*. Two of my three friends were married. One had been dating for under a year. They envied me as I felt pangs of guilt for revealing the innermost sanctum of our little mystery cult of two.

They say that all of us live three lives: a public; a private; and a secret life. Where is my life with Lo? It's secret, on one level. But not secret to each other. It's private, between the two of us. Yet we publish it for all to see. Our most intimate parts are literally on display for the world.

Revealing who we are to you, our dear readers, is one thing. Saying it directly, face-to-face to close, and long-time friends of flesh-and-blood is another. They know the public, curated portrait of our coupled relationship. That image is professional, wholesome, vanilla. We do little to 'queer the space,' as the saying goes.

Privately, we are a kinky couple who invite others to join in with our merry mischief. We are content doing this and feel no shame, no guilt about healthy, non-monogamous trysts. Lo simply acts on the fantasies that many women share, but rarely articulate, even to their lovers.

Secretly, we each find delight in her exhibitionist tendencies. That's no secret to you, dear reader, but, if you happen to know us IRL ('in real life'), we'd appreciate your keeping it to yourself. Thanks.

But now, three of my closest friends were in on it. Not as in on it as you are, mind you, since I didn't reveal to them anything about the blog. But they were in the know about Lo's sweet, sexy, slutty side. To my surprise, they were not only envious, but desirous. Each of them requested a night alone with my phone. Since there was no wi-fi, I thought it would be fine. They couldn't email themselves Lo's sexy pics. They couldn't text them to themselves. What harm would there be in letting my three friends get their rocks off to my girlfriend's nude selfies?

It turns out I was quite naïve. At the time, I knew nothing of "AirDrop" and how it could work without wi-fi. Needless to say, all three of my friends now have Lo's sexy pics on their phones and who knows how many other friends of theirs as well! (I only found this out much later.)

Fishing, drinking, and jacking off to Lola was how we spent the rest of the week.

On the ride home, as soon as I was reconnected to the invisible world that surrounds us, I texted Lo. I let her know my ETA. She responded with: "TCB." That is, "Taking Care of

Business," our code for her masturbating. I couldn't wait to see her.

The guys dropped me off at home and I eagerly entered the house. I found Lo wearing my flannel shirt, unbuttoned to her navel, and nothing else. What a welcome sight!

I followed her to the bedroom, telling her how wonderful she looked. Eager to preserve the moment, I took out the camera and shot a few sexy pics of her lying on the bed looking like the perfect temptress.

"Tell me about your week, Daddio," she asked.

"Later. Let me have you first," I said, impatiently.

"Oh, but Daddio, I haven't heard from you all week. Tell me about it."

"Later, Lo," I pleaded. "I want you now."

She was clearly enjoying the role reversal of Coy and Craving.

I started to grab at her. "You know, I'm not fast food. You can't just order and have your meal."

"Let me spread my mayonnaise on you," I said.

"Oh Daddio, so crude!"

"Lo, you don't understand."

"I'm not really into it right now," she said. She was truly going to milk this for all she could, and not in a good way.

"But I'll get you into it by getting into you!"

"No, no," she said like a coquette. "Tell me about your fishing trip."

"Let me plunge my fishing rod deep in your C," I responded.

Then it struck me with great irony that here I am, a writer of erotica, rushing to physical gratification when all Lo wanted was to be wooed by my words. She wanted me to tell her a naughty story. And fortuitously, I had a good story to tell.

I got up close next to her and told her about how much I missed her, how I longed for her, how I gazed at her photos while writing stories about her, and how I got found out by the guys. I revealed that her seductive image was used not only by me but by the other three as well. Though it clearly upset her to know that they had seen her, it also excited her to know that they used her photos to get off. Cognitive dissonance.

"Do you think that they stole my photos and have them on their phones?" she asked.

"How could they?" I responded. "There was no wi-fi."

"Oh," she said, sounding disappointed. "If they did, do you think that they'd look at them at night while their wives were sleeping?"

"I'm sure of it."

"Do you think that when they see me, they'll picture me naked?"

"Not only that, I bet they'll picture you doing all sorts of naughty things."

"Like what things?" she asked.

"Sucking cock."

"Just one?"

"Sucking cocks," I said, correcting myself. "Fucking many guys. Dogging strangers at truck rest stops."

She was getting riled up now.

"Have me, Daddy," she said.

Finally! The words I longed to hear all week!

She spread her legs wide, but then she said, "Wait," just as I was about to plunge in.

"What?"

"Wait," she repeated. "Do you have a condom?"

"A condom? No. Why?"

"I'm ovulating something fierce right now."

"I'll be careful."

"No. You've been on the wagon for a week. You're not to be trusted."

"I haven't slipped a puck passed the goalie yet."

"Will you stop with that awful analogy."

She had her hands behind her knees and her knees up to her ears. She looked up at me. She wanted me, desperately. I wanted her even more desperately. She moved one of her hands to grab my cock. She bounced the tip of it off her clit a few times and let out a moan.

"Are we good?" I asked.

"Jack it," she commanded.

"I could have jacked it all week. I want *you*."

"What do you mean you could have jacked it all week? Not without permission you can't," she said, reminding me of the rules.

"But you gave me permission, remember? You said I could jack it so long as I jacked it to your pics and only your pics. That was the whole reason that we took those sexy pics that the guys found on my phone."

"And you didn't jack it?"

"No."

"Not to me? Not to my pics?"

"No."

"Why not?"

"Because I wanted you. I looked to your pics for inspiration. I wrote like three novels up there about you, just gazing at your sexy photos."

"But they jacked it to my pics?"

"Yes."

Just the thought of it caused her to squirt on my incredibly hard phallus.

"Jack it," she said again. I could see that the image in her mind of guys jacking off to her photos was playing on her interior screen. "Jack it like a man," she repeated.

I grabbed my cock with my left hand. She watched me. "Do you like my pussy, Daddy?"

"Yes, Lo."

"Play with it."

I didn't know if she wanted me to play with my cock or her puss. It was ambiguous.

I let go of my member and she continued to hold both her legs back with her hands. I gently caressed her hips and slid my hands down from the back of her knees to her inner thigh. With both hands I pulled and pushed her pussy lips – spreading them apart, squeezing them together.

"Yeah," she moaned. She squirted on my hands and the warm liquid dribbled down her ass. I let my fingers strum her perineum and anus. She moaned, indicating she liked what I was doing. I let my right thumb run circles over her special spot.

"I missed you, Daddy," she said.

"Did you jill it when I was away?"

"Yes," she said.

"How many times?"

"I don't know. A lot."

"To what?"

"I don't know. Anything. Everything. Sometimes I thought about you. Sometimes I thought about other men. Sometimes I thought about other women. Videos, pics that people send me, stories that you wrote, stories that other people wrote."

"Did you talk on the phone to anyone?"

"No Daddy."

"Did you have anyone over?"

"No Daddy."

"Did you want to?"

"I always want to, Daddy."

She came again. She slapped her right hand on her pussy to keep the ejaculation flowing. Then she took her soaking hand and stroked my cock.

"Does it hurt?" she asked.

"Yes."

She reached down, up and under my cock, grabbing my balls from beneath.

"They're so big, Daddy. Are they full?"

"So full, Lo," I said.

She cupped them and one of her fingers pushed its way further back until she was doing to me what I had been doing to her.

"Cum, Daddy. I want you to cum. Let it out. That's it. Be a good dog and let it go."

I could take it no longer. I grabbed my throbbing rod and fired off a load that shot up past her shoulder onto the pillow. Missed. But the second spurt was more accurate. It made a high arc and landed squarely on her face. Seeing that, more followed until I was falling back on my haunches in a fit of ecstasy and exhaustion.

"I'm hit! I'm hit!" she cried out. "Don't just lie there, do something!"

All I could do was let out a chuckle amid my heavy heaving breaths.

She got up from the bed, my cum dripping down onto her breasts, and got a washcloth from the bathroom to clean up.

"Feeling better?" she asked as she looked down at me from the side of the bed.

"You have no idea," I said.

Sherry Rain

I looked down and I saw Lola's finger gently stroking Stoya's pussy. She slid her wet finger up and down the soft labia and then gently inserted one, then two fingers deep inside. "You like this, Daddy? You want to fuck her pussy?" she asked. I did, but for the moment I was enjoying the view as I held my cock in my hands.

Now, allow me to tell you how we arrived at that supremely sexy moment.

It was late August. Lo and I packed up our big cooler full of beers, G&T, and various snack items: salsa, hummus, cheeses. We had a picnic basket full of chips, pita bread, pretzels, and basically everything you could want as an appetizer, but no meal.

We got on the road early. We knew that the parking spots at the beach would fill up quick since the weather forecast for that Saturday was so perfect and we knew that there wouldn't be many more opportunities to get to the ocean this summer.

All the way out there, Lo was in high spirits. In summer she loves three things: heat, beach, and picnic baskets. Well, and sex. Don't forget the sex.

I just like seeing her in her bikini (and out of her bikini).

We got there just in time to get one of the few remaining spots in the parking lot and I carried the heavy stuff while Lo rolled the cooler. We set up the chairs and umbrella, spread out the beach blanket, and I pulled out a book and sat in the chair surveying the area while Lo lay spread eagle on the blanket.

"On the B.P.?" Lo asked me. That's our abbreviation for either "Beach Patrol," or, more accurately, "Butt Patrol."

There were a few couples around us, but we were in the mostly vacant far end of the beach, away from the crowds and screaming children.

The hours spent soaking up the sun sped by as Lo and I sipped our cold drinks and nibbled on the provisions. I got a good chunk of reading done, swam a few times when I got too hot to bake any longer, and enjoyed seeing Lo apply and reapply her sunscreen.

When the sun was low on the horizon, Lo and I packed up our temporary home in the sand, put it all in the trunk and then headed off to one of our favorite restaurants, right on the water.

We walked up to the rooftop bar and, though it was crowded, we managed to snag the last high-top table for two overlooking the blue water below and the sunset in the distance. It was perfect. We were famished and already feeling the effects of day-drinking while sunbathing.

We ate our meal as the band played "Margaritaville" and other classic summer songs. Lo's feet kept rubbing up on my legs. I could tell what she was hungry for now and I was eager to get her home to feed it to her.

We paid the bill and just as we stood to leave, we heard someone from the next table say, "Oh, don't go yet!" Was that directed at us? I turned around and saw two women sitting at one of the other high-top tables. Rather than sit across from one another, as Lo and I had been sitting in order to see each other, they both sat on one side of the small table, and they were looking at us. My back was to them the whole time, but had Lo seen them? I don't know.

"What?" I asked, politely, but a bit defensively.

"Don't go yet," one of them repeated. Apparently, they enjoyed looking at us.

"Why's that?" I asked.

"Never mind her," said the other woman in a deeper voice, "we've been here all day and now she's drunk."

"I am not!" the first protested.

"Whatever," said the second.

We were in no hurry. We had been together all day and something about these two women appealed to us (or appealed to our vanity), so we took a seat on the other side of the table. We began with introductions. The taller, deeper voiced woman was Sherry, and the smaller, sandy-haired woman's name was Rain. They were a couple. They had been together for about a year, and they admitted to watching the two of us.

We ordered another round of drinks, even though Lo and I had already settled for our dinner.

"You have amazing tits," said Rain. She was either less reserved than Sherry, or much more drunk. I couldn't tell since I knew them not at all.

Lo almost blushed, but not quite. She was still in her bikini top and shorts.

"She has a great ass too," I chimed in.

"I bet," said Rain, liking her lips. The gesture reminded me of Lo's trademark move and when I looked over at Lo, it was like a mirror reflection of Rain. They clearly had chemistry. I looked at Sherry whose poker face was inscrutable. Did she enjoy the flirting, as I did, or resent it? Was this just another night out for this interesting couple, or was Rain playing a dangerous game?

No matter, it wasn't my relationship at stake.

We continued drinking and finding out more about the two of them. Rain was a yoga instructor. Sherry worked in finance. an odd couple, for sure.

The band continued to play and at some point, after we had had another round or two, they played Bob Marley's "Three Little Birds."

"I *love* this song!" Rain informed us as she jumped off her barstool and grabbed Lo's hand saying, "Dance with me!" She almost dragged her onto the dancefloor in her enthusiasm. The two of them swayed back and forth and Rain put her hands on Lo's hips as Lo put her arms around Rain's waist. I could see their lips moving, but not hear what they said. I realized that I wasn't the only one watching them. Not only were the other folks in the bar glued to these two long-haired, sexy beach babes dancing, but Sherry was also eyeing them closely. I decided to use the opportunity of our being mutually abandoned to try to understand what was going on for her.

"She always this friendly?" I asked.

A tense smile hid her frustration. "Rain? She's a very free spirit," she said. It was meant to sound like a compliment, but it came across as a complaint.

"Same with Lo," I said, genuinely, "that's why I love her so."

She smiled again and I decided to lighten the mood a bit. "You have great teeth."

"Oh," she said, surprised, clearly not used to being complimented, "thanks."

One little observation goes a long way. After that, she really opened up to me, telling me more about her and Rain.

The band played another song and Lo and Rain kept dancing. I saw Rain move her hand to Lo's butt, over her denim shorts. Their bodies moved closer together, their steps smaller.

Sherry told me that this was her first relationship with a woman. She was newly divorced. She had two kids – teenagers. They were very conflicted about everything. I could see that either their emotions reflected her own or she was projecting. She and Rain had only been together about a year and a half. Rain had never been with a man, but was fascinated by men ... and afraid of them.

Sherry was just as intoxicated as Rain, I realized, only she hid it better. She hid, or tried to hide, a lot of things. She went on to tell me that she's often caught Rain masturbating to porn of guys jackin' it and cumming. "She's fascinated by guys ejaculating," she said as if it was the most bizarre thing for a lesbian to be curious about. "She watches it again and again."

Lo and Rain came back from the dance floor.

"At least someone dances with me," Lo said, jibing me for my reluctance to set foot on any dance floor.

"At least someone talks to me," I said, looking at Sherry.

"Oh yeah," asked Rain, "what were you two talking about?"

"If I tell you," I said, "you'll tell me how nice Lo's ass is."

"Deal!" she said.

I looked at Sherry and saw real fear in her eyes. Of course, I wasn't going to publicize her intimate revelation. "We were just talking about Sherry's kids and how quickly they grow up."

"I know! Right?" said Rain, "When I met them, I was taller than both of them. But now they're both this tall," she said, putting her hand above her head by a foot.

Sherry looked relieved.

We talked some more, got some appetizers and more beer. Lo and I opened up about our special relationship. When Rain heard that I'm not allowed to have the same freedoms as Lo, she suddenly became more interested in me. It was as if being off limits was a dare for her, a challenge, a goal. She was now openly flirting with both Lo and me.

I completely lost track of time, but I knew we had a long drive home. We got the check, exchanged numbers, and said that we all need to come back here again together before the summer was over.

We walked downstairs and out onto the sidewalk. Their destination was the opposite direction from ours. Lo gave a hug to Sherry as I went in to give a goodbye hug to Rain, but to my great astonishment, rather than a hug, Rain's lips came in right for mine. This was no little, polite peck goodnight, but an open-mouthed kiss, full of lips-on-lips and tongue exploration. She hugged me close and squeezed and the thought occurred to me that she was squeezing me as she wanted to be squeezed.

When our embrace ended, I furtively looked over to Lo to see just how much trouble I was in now. But Lo was busy talking with Sherry. Had either of them seen what just went down? Then Lo came over to Rain to give her a very proper and polite hug goodbye while I hugged Sherry. There were no hard feelings, or at least none that I could detect.

Lo and I began walking along the dimly lit sidewalk next to the dark beach. In our spirited conversation with the women, apparently Lo forgot the most important thing to do before departing a bar.

"Daddy," she said, "I have to go to the bathroom."

"What?"

"I have to pee. So bad."

"Well, let's go back. You can ..."

She cut me off. "No," she said, "why should we go all the way back when we have all the beach to ourselves?"

"What?" I asked, astonished as I saw Lo walk onto the sandy beach, pull down and remove her shorts but leaving on her bikini bottoms as she stuck out her bum like she was grinding into the invisible groin of someone in a dance club.

"Are you peeing?" I asked in disbelief.

"Come here and I'll show you," she said, grabbing my wrist, pulling my hand between her legs so I could feel the drips as they seeped through her bottoms.

"Lo," I gasped, "you're bad!"

"You love it," she said. "You know you do."

She wasn't wrong.

"OK," she said, "let's go."

She grabbed me so we walked arm-in-arm and she sashayed down the sidewalk.

"Feel better, dear?"

"Much," she said. "Feel hard, dear?" she asked as she reached over to feel my cock under my bathing suit. "Oh yeah," she said, answering her own question, "you feel hard alright."

She wasn't wrong.

We got to the car and I got in, but I called to Lo before she got in. "Hey, you plan on taking off your bottoms?"

"What?"

"Your bottoms. Do you plan on taking them off?"

"Here? On the street?"

"Yes here, on the street. You certainly don't plan on sitting on my car seat like that do you?"

"Like what, Daddy?" she asked innocently.

"Drenched in pee."

"Drenched in pee?! What are you talking about?"

"Your little trinkle on the beach."

"What?"

"You honestly don't remember?"

"No. Is that why I'm all wet? I just thought I was really horny. I mean, I *am* really horny, but is that why I'm wet?"

"Yes. So strip."

"This sounds like a fun ride," she said as she dropped her bikini bottoms onto the sidewalk, threw them in the trunk, and got in the car.

I started up the engine and she reached over to grab my cock. "Do you want me to straddle you, Daddy?" she asked.

"No, Lo, I'm driving home."

"Can I blow you?"

"No."

"Hand job?"

"No."

"Well, what am I supposed to do for this long ride home?" she asked as she put her bare feet up on the dashboard, spreading them to make a 'V' of her legs. "Just look at what you've got here," she said as she slapped her cleanly shaved pussy.

She put the seat all the way back and reclined it as far as it would go, keeping her feet up on the dash as she began massaging her pussy. But within mere moments she was sound asleep next to me.

The first half of the ride home was fine since we were on the highway. But once we got off the highway, there were red lights, and I could see the guys in the cars next to us looking at Lo. At one point a pickup truck was stopped next to me. The driver looked down at her naked body and then at me and he gave me a thumbs-up sign. I took my shirt off and threw it over Lo's bare mons pubis, but, in her sleep, she grabbed it and used it as a pillow. Even when passed out she is an inveterate exhibitionist!

We got home and I roused her. It took a great deal of effort, but I finally got her out of the car and up the stairs of our apartment building, all butt naked.

Once in our apartment, she crawled into bed. Now she was waking up.

"Fuck me, Daddy," she said, spreading her legs.

"Lo, you're beyond the ability to consent."

"No, I'm not, Daddy," she protested. "Don't you want me?"

"I sure do, but I'm not having you," I replied.

"Please?"

"No."

"Then I guess I'll have to take things into my own hands," she said, pulling out her dildo from under the bed and swiftly inserting it between her legs.

"If you're going to do that," I countered, "then I'm going to have some fun too. You're not the only one with toys anymore."

I rummaged through the closet and found my Stoya Fleshlight.

"No, Daddy! You wouldn't dare!" she cried, still masturbating. "You wouldn't have her when you could have me, would you?"

"Lo, I'm not having you."

She grabbed Stoya from my hands and began touching her pussy lips.

"You can lubricate her for me, if you want," I said.

She put out her hand and took some lube from the bottle as I squeezed it into her palm.

She stroked the pussy gently as I held my love organ in my hands.

"You like fingering her?" I asked.

No response.

"Are you thinking of Rain right now?"

"How'd you know?" she asked.

I was standing next to the bed as I watched all of this happening. Then Lo slid so that her legs were dangling off the side of the bed. With one hand she kept the dildo rhythmically fucking her pussy and with the other hand she slid Stoya's pussy over my rock-hard cock.

"You like that, Daddy?"

Now I didn't answer.

She went back and forth with the Fleshlight, fucking my cock with it as she fucked herself with her dildo.

"That's it, Daddy, fuck her. Fuck her like you'd fuck me," she said until she squirted all over the wood floor next to the bed. At the sight of her ejaculation, I grabbed Stoya with both hands and fucked Stoya hard and fast. Lo reached down, underneath and held my balls. She likes to feel them contract when I ejaculate. I came and came a lot inside Stoya.

After we cleaned everything up, Lo lay in my arms. She fell right to sleep. I held her and thought of the sound of the waves gently rolling over the silent sand of the beach in the moonlight.

About Lola & H.H.

Based in the US, The Tempestuous Tandem of Lola and H.H. pushes the boundaries of conventional relationships, captivating readers and followers with their unapologetic exploration of desire and the endless possibilities of a love that knows no limits. Volume 6: Slut Life from the Match, Cinder & Spark series is their first publication with Erosetti Press. Their blog, books, and audiobooks have attracted a large underground, nearly cultish, following. Lola Down, the "average nympho next door," has inspired tribute artwork and photos from readers around the world. Her fans often like to display themselves with the books in equally evocative ways, hoping to stimulate Lo to even more exciting "sexcapades." These fan images and art are published along with the stories in the books and on their active blog and social media. Lola and H.H. are at the center of a community of erotic art and expression, and we are proud to partner with them to bring you their latest book! You can engage with them on their blog site mysexlifewithlola.com and their X and Instagram social media.

More from Erosetti Press

The Anthology of Erotic Narrative, Volume II Illustrated by Ester Cardella
Ten international authors present erotic exploring the extremes of desire and fantasy, with uncensored illustrations by renown Palermo artist Ester Cardella.

The Anthology of Erotic Narrative, Volume I Fetish

Featuring international authors and illustrations by fetish artist Coax, these stories unflinchingly push of boundaries of eroticism into new realms of bondage and desire.

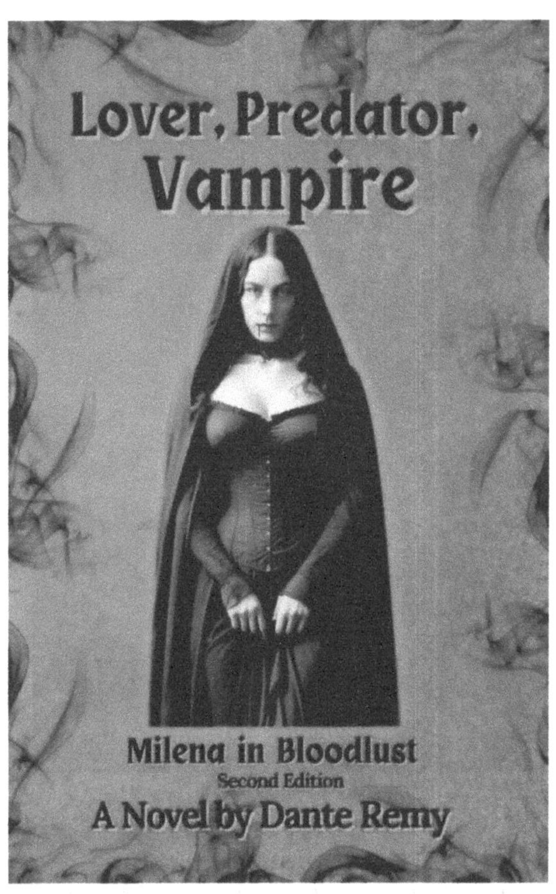

Lover, Predator, Vampire
Blood and lust mingle with folklore in this
new take on the vampire story, told in the
voice of Milena, a heroine femme fatale
ahead of her time.

The Mysteries,
I Misteri del Convento

A bold and transformative exploration of desire, faith, and surrender, blending historical erotica with spiritual awakening in a story that dares to illuminate the sacred power of the forbidden. Illustrated by world renown erotic artist Apollonia Saintclair.

Carmilla

The essential sapphic, erotic, vampire classic, now restored with the original serialized illustrations, period artwork, and a forward for curated reading experience.

9 781968 703110